Does the stranger know Bessie's secret?

His smile drew creases all around his eyes and then he turned his attention toward Bessie, as William made the introductions.

"Joe Robertson. A neighbor and a good friend."

Joe held out his big hand. Bessie's first instinct was to back away, but she was already tight against the shelves, so she allowed her hand to disappear into his warm, hard grasp.

"I was sorry to hear about your loss." She was forced to look into his face. Eyes so black they appeared to have no pupils bored into hers. She felt herself spiraling downward—or was it upward? She couldn't tell for, inwardly, she had lost her balance. His expression never faltered from that of a kind stranger, but she was sure he had seen right into her soul—seen her pain and guilt, and she longed to get out of the room and find a place to hide, someplace where she could escape this man with the knowing eyes.

LINDA FORD draws on her own observations of the Canadian prairie for this inspiring story. She lives with her family in Alberta, where she is also a member of the Alberta Romance Writers Association.

Don't miss out on any of our super romances. Write to us at the following address for information on our newest releases and club information.

Heartsong Presents Readers' Service
P.O. Box 719
Uhrichsville, OH 44683

The Sun
Still Shines

Linda Ford

Heartsong Presents

Gratefully and lovingly dedicated to those who helped me reach my dream: Andrea, Shawna, Marcia, and members of the Alberta Romance Writers Association who provided encouragement and needed critiquing; to my family who gave me the freedom to write; and especially to my husband who believed in my dream.

A note from the author:
I love to hear from my readers! You may write to me at the following address: **Linda Ford**
Author Relations
P.O. Box 719
Uhrichsville, OH 44683

ISBN 1-57748-155-0

THE SUN STILL SHINES

Cover illustration by Lorraine Bush.

PRINTED IN THE U.S.A.

one

The sky was an inverted bowl of azure blue over a tableland of yellowed grass that bent and bowed in the moaning wind.

The relentless wind.

Bessie Macleod tightened the ribbons under her chin and choked back her rushing anxiety.

"How much farther?" she asked her brother, William, who was sitting beside her, driving the wagon.

As if her words had stirred him into action, he pulled the reins and slowed the wagon, turning off the twin tracks toward a bluff of trees. "We'll stop here for some lunch," he said, calling, "Whoa," to the animals. Jumping from the wagon, he left Bessie to make her own way down.

She sighed and stretched her arms stiffly. She had noticed the way William's eyes widened when he saw her at the station last night. He still thought of her as a gawky half-grown girl just beginning to show signs of maturing. The Bessie he had last seen back home three years ago would have jumped from the wagon before him and beat him to the picnic Mother set out.

Only Mother wasn't here to spread a picnic. It would be left to Bessie to take care of such details.

She straightened slowly. The numbness in her bottom sharpened to needle points then gave way to a slow steady ache. Her limbs responded unwillingly as she scrambled over the edge of the wagon and lurched to the rough ground.

Picking up her skirts she stumbled to the back of the wagon to check on Robert. Her husband lay against the packing crates, his cheeks as pale as the old dead grass at her feet. The past few days had not only sucked the color from his cheeks, they seemed to have drawn away the flesh as well. Although still handsome, his face looked old and sunken. Bessie clamped her

5

teeth and refused to admit he looked worse now than when they began the trip.

He must get better. He must.

A twiggy branch of some long-dead weed caught at her skirts before it skittered away and tangled in the spokes of the wheel. It clung even as it flapped and fluttered.

Shuddering, Bessie gaped at the struggling weed praying it would stay anchored to the wheel.

Life is so uncertain, she thought. *There is nothing to hold on to.*

Nothing but Robert, who seemed weaker than ever.

Blinking his eyes as he struggled awake, Robert began to cough. Bright spots stained his cheeks and sweat beaded on his brow.

William reached into the wagon and pulled out a jug. "Here's water," he said, uncorking it.

The coughing stopped as Robert sipped from his tin cup.

Relief made Bessie's knees shake. Every time he had a coughing spell, she held her breath, willing him to find ease. Every time, she demanded of the universe why he should have to suffer. Why she should be made to feel so vulnerable.

While William returned to tending the animals, Robert helped Bessie spread the grey blanket on the ground, raising the musty smell of old grass.

Bessie turned her back to the wind, letting her skirts wrap around her legs. "Robert," she murmured, "It's so big." Her eyes swept the prairie, taking in the green beginning to show through last summer's grass, the sweep of the land. Rolling, rolling, rolling until it disappeared into the distant horizon. "I haven't seen a house for ages."

Pulling her to his side, he nodded. "But feel the sun." Closing his eyes, he lifted his face heavenward. "It warms me right to my bones."

Bessie sighed so quietly it was barely audible. She knew the trip was necessary. She had reconciled herself to it and to her duty as a well-trained young woman to obediently follow her husband wherever he went. Her upbringing had prepared her to be both dutiful and obedient.

It had not prepared her for this.

"Where are the people?" she asked.

"We're here. That's all that matters. We'll soon be at William's place and can get settled."

Bessie remembered William had not answered when she asked how much farther. Her eyes searched the open field. She had so many questions.

Were there neighbors? It was not a question that had crossed her mind when they set out, but the last few hours had made it increasingly urgent.

How long before she and Robert could return to Toronto?

Could she be happy here?

She knew how to make the routine of daily living run smoothly, but no one had told her how to still the inner arguments that raged as she silently complied with decisions in which she had no part.

Taking a long, steadying breath, she reminded herself that she could have offered no alternative to this trip if she had been asked. The agony of watching Robert grow weaker as the days passed had prepared her to accept anything that would restore his health.

It wasn't fair! Someone as good and kind and intelligent as Robert should not be so weak he couldn't sit at his desk and work.

How often had she screamed those words inside her head, never sharing her fear and anger with anyone? Not even Robert. Robert, who frequently guessed her thoughts and put a voice to them before she was able to find the right words, never guessed how afraid she was of losing him.

Or did he?

Even now his arm tightened around her and she felt strength pour from his weakened body into her trembling heart.

She turned and looked at his face, fearing he had guessed her anxious thoughts, but his eyes were still closed, his face raised as he breathed slowly. Slipping away, she opened a box and set out the lunch of cold biscuits and hard-boiled eggs, sulfur fumes twitching her nostrils as Robert cracked open a shell.

"William," Robert began as her brother rejoined them, "Bessie says she hasn't seen any homes for a while. I thought the country was getting settled."

William turned startled eyes to Bessie. "Why, we passed the Sloan place not more than twenty minutes ago." He shrugged. "Maybe you didn't notice it. It's pretty well hidden from the road. Before that there was Crawford's and the Swedes', and just over the hill there's a whole passel of Norwegians."

"I didn't see them."

"The land's settling up pretty good," William went on as if she hadn't spoken. *Still having trouble believing I'm no longer a child,* she thought. "Fact is, some say it's getting too crowded. I heard Old Man Burridges just up and sold his place and moved away. Too many people to suit him."

Bessie stared at the empty space around her. As far as she could she there was no dwelling place. No sign of life apart from the crows and gophers. How could anyone say it was getting too crowded? She scanned the horizon again longing for some sign of human habitation, but saw none. There was nothing as far as the eye could see. The bigness of the land and its emptiness filled her heart with a coiling emotion she couldn't identify.

"It's good of you to invite us to stay with you," Robert said. He and William had not met before last night. "I hope we won't be. . ." He had a coughing fit and couldn't go on.

Bessie rubbed his back knowing it would do little to relieve the cough, but needing to touch him and somehow share his struggle.

"We'll manage fine, I'm sure," said William when Robert's breathing came easy again.

"It won't be for long," Bessie assure him. "As soon as Robert's better we'll return to Toronto." And to a normal life, to building our home and our future together. Their future had seemed bright with promise eight months ago when they married. Now here she was, an eighteen-year old, almost new bride travelling thousands of miles to live with her brother in Alberta.

Alberta. Even the name sounded lonesome and strange.

"Well, I'll stretch my legs a bit, then we best be on our way." William strode toward the trees.

"Bess, get my bag will you?" Hurrying to the wagon, she pulled out his travel case. Robert's eyes glowed with eagerness as he drew out his journal. "I'll catch up while we wait." Already his head was bent over the page.

Gathering up the lunch things, Bessie wondered what Robert could find noteworthy in their surroundings. Sky. Wind. Grass. Caw. Caw. Caw.

The silence settled around them buzzing in her ears like the sound of a million bees. She wanted to press her hands to her ears, curl up into a little ball, and wait for this to end.

Robert lay on the grass, a finger in his book, his eyes shut. She moved closer, letting his presence anchor her against the emptiness tearing at her senses.

"The sun feels so good," he murmured, eyes still closed.

"I thought you had fallen asleep." She stroked the fine sand-colored hair off his brow, missing the silky strands that had given way to dull lanks.

"No, I'm just enjoying the sunshine." He took her hand and pressed it to his chest and when she leaned forward to kiss him, he pulled her down, tucking her into the hollow at his side.

She snuggled in, listening to his breathing. Did it come easier than it had? She stifled her own disquieting thoughts. She would endure anything if it made Robert better. Anything, she admonished herself. Even this frightening emptiness.

"Humph." William cleared his throat. "Best be on our way."

Bessie scrambled to her feet, tucking Robert's journal back into his bag and carrying it to the back of the wagon. As Robert climbed in and settled himself between the crates, Bessie shook the coarse grey blanket, scattering bits of yellowed grass in the wind. She wrapped it around Robert's legs, then climbed up next to William on the seat, which felt harder with every bounce.

William flicked the reins and clucked to the horses. She waited until the wagon was back on the trail and William slouched over the reins before she turned to him. "How much farther, William?"

❧

Soon, he'd said. *Soon.*

Still the wagon rattled on, jolting over the rough ground, the protesting creak of the wood echoing the inner cry of her bones. A flock of wild chickens rose before them, their wings beating the silence.

Robert crawled forward to the seat. "Seems to be a lot of wildlife around. I've seen a number of creatures I'm unfamiliar with."

"Those were Hungarian Partridges," William said.

"And those little deer-like animals?"

"Pronghorn antelope."

Robert fell silent, and Bessie knew he was mentally preparing notes for his journal.

She closed her eyes to shut out the rolling plains. She didn't care about the animals or the flowers and trees Robert asked William to identify. She needed to see people. Where were the people?

Leaning on the back of the seat, Robert pressed his face against her arm. "It's beautiful, isn't it, Bessie?"

She studied her twenty-five year old husband. The trip had been hard on him. The dust in the train, and the poor accommodations all showed in the hollows in his cheeks, but the dullness in his eyes had been replaced by an eagerness she hadn't seen for a long time, since he had fallen ill right after Christmas. If this forsaken land could do that to him she would be eternally grateful. "Yes," she finally answered. "It's beautiful." She meant its healing power while Robert meant the land itself, but it didn't matter. Anything that restored his health was truly beautiful in her eyes.

"That's Ryanville in the distance," William said. Bessie knew his place was close to Ryanville and she sat up straight and stared. "I don't see anything," she said after a moment of concentrated study.

"Over to the side a bit." William pointed. "And not so high."

Bessie lowered her gaze and stared again. Her stomach wrenched in a gripping spasm. Surely he didn't mean those few scattered buildings! But there was nothing else.

She held herself rigid, waiting for the twisting in her middle to pass, waiting for William to drive on. Instead, he turned toward the buildings.

"So this is Ryanville," she said, not realizing she was speaking aloud until William answered her.

"This is it." His voice rang with a note of satisfaction. He slowed down to pass the buildings. "There's Mr. Scofield's new office. I built it during the winter."

The squat building gleamed with new lumber. Mr. Scofield's name was lettered across the window in square, black letters. The window blushed rosy in the late afternoon sun and winked as they passed.

"That's the store." William pointed across Bessie. A large wooden sign said, "Waley's General Store."

"He carries a good line of merchandise."

"Is he married?" Bessie asked.

"Nope. He and his mother live in quarters behind the store."

"How about Mr. Scofield?"

"He's an old bachelor. There's the livery barn, the feed mill, the ladies shop," William continued with his cheerful tour.

The town was ready to click shut after them. Bessie's muscles tensed as she stared at the lonely, empty land looming beyond the wide street. There was nothing in this town for her.

The clucking of chickens jerked her attention back from the vast emptiness. Behind an unpainted picket fence a handful of chickens shared the yard with two children. Hungrily, Bessie stared at the children, noting the pile of dirt between them and the spoon each child held. The older, a boy, scooped dirt from a hole in front of him and added it to the pile. The other, a girl in a soiled blue dress with a smudge of dirt on her right cheek, turned toward the wagon and waved. Choking back a sob, Bessie returned the wave. Life. Children. It wasn't all old men and old women, bachelors and hermits.

"Who lives there?" she asked, turning to keep her eyes on the children as the wagon rattled past.

"The Pedersons. He farms this quarter." William waved to her right.

Here was hope for a friend. These young children had a mother, perhaps someone close to her age. She hugged the knowledge close to her heart, but before she could ask William for more details, Robert spoke.

"There seems to be a lot of growth in Ryanville. I noticed six new buildings." She should have known he would be itemizing all the details.

Nodding, William agreed. "I've been working in town for several months. Lots of people moving in. And there's talk of the railway coming through."

"What does Mr. Scofield do?" Robert was still mentally sorting things into slots.

"He registers land titles and runs a small bank."

"There's no lawyer?" Robert asked. Bessie wondered if he wanted a fellow lawyer to talk to, or someone from whom he could borrow books. As if they hadn't brought enough. Four of the boxes were Robert's books and it had been almost more than he could do to pick the ones he would leave behind.

"It's only for a little while," she had reminded him, but he looked so mournful at the thought of leaving them for even a short time she had laughed and teased him. "You'd think they were your children."

He laughed at those words and kissed her. "I confess I love them, but they're more like friends than children. When we have children, I'll never be away from them."

Bessie knew how he felt about a family. He wanted a whole houseful of children, robust and healthy, running in and out, laughing and playing. It was because he'd had such a lonely, quiet existence as a child, due in part to the fact he was an only child, and in part, because he was so often ill. Robert had told her how he envied the other children who passed his window every day on their way to school. How strong and rowdy there were. He longed to have children of his own and enjoy their pleasures with them.

"My place is just around that little knoll," William announced and the horses increased their pace as if anxious to be home.

The harnesses rattled like bells, cheering them on the way, and Bessie strained forward, waiting to catch a glimpse of her new home.

The horses snorted, and without guidance from the reins, turned into a narrow, dusty lane. Bessie clutched the edge of the seat. The trees cast long shadows over the trail and gloom clung to the hollows.

"Welcome to my place." William's voice deepened with pride. "I hope you'll be happy." He paused briefly then added in a lower note. "And well."

There was little to indicate this was a farm. A few yards away squatted a low, dark structure, surrounded by a rail fence. That would be the barn, she thought as the horses tossed their heads and strained toward it, but she searched in vain for another building. Turning to William, her voice tight with apprehension, she said, "I don't see a house."

William clucked the horses forward a few more steps then jumped down. "Did you forget I live in a sod shack?" He lifted boxes from the wagon and set them before a weathered wooden door stuck in the side of a hill.

Bessie swallowed and stared. She swallowed again.

A soddie, he had written and she never thought any more of it. A soddie seemed to be made of strips of dirt and grass. She should have figured that out, but it hadn't seemed important. She was so certain William would have adequate living quarters. After all, he was a good carpenter. That's why he had come west—because of the call for good carpenters.

From the outside, the soddie looked like a pile of freshly turned soil with squared edges. Bessie couldn't tear her eyes away from it. All she could think of were the spiders and bugs that live in dark, cold places. She shuddered. As a child, whenever Mother sent her to the basement, Bessie had pulled a scarf over her head, and she would shake her skirts and stomp her feet when she returned. The thought of a spider crawling on her made her teeth rattle. She could not possibly share a hole in the ground with the creepy, crawly insects. They were quite welcome to keep it to themselves.

"Come, Bessie," Robert took her hand and urged her off the wagon. He kept her hand in his even after she stood facing the browned, water-streaked door. "I'm sure we'll find it quite adequate. We'll get settled and we'll soon be comfortable." His voice was low and soothing, and Bessie knew he had seen her shock and was trying to help her gain control.

Behind her she heard the stomp and snort of the horses, restless to be released, and she heard William's grunt as he lifted another box from the wagon followed by a thud as he dropped it on the ground next to the others.

Bessie swallowed again and tried to speak but her constricted throat allowed only a weak squeak. She clutched Robert's hand and stared at the straight walls of dirt. She lifted her eyes to the roof. Last year's grass, yellowed and bent, lay several inches above her head. No wonder the shack looked like it was part of the hill.

William elbowed past them. "I'll light the lantern then you can have a look around." He disappeared inside the dark interior and returned almost instantly, surrounded by a golden glow. "Come in. Come in." He stepped aside and waved his arm. His eyes met Bessie's and she knew he was waiting for a sign that his home met her approval, but she raised her eyes and stared at the dark interior beyond his shoulders. Her limbs froze and a great weight pressed against her chest. She could not speak despite the beseeching way William watched her. Nor could she move as Robert took a step forward, urging her to follow.

She stood on a narrow ledge; behind her the vast lonely emptiness of the prairies; in front, the closeness of the dark sod shanty. She was trapped. There was no escape.

two

Bessie forced herself to take a deep breath as Mother's words came to her. How often Mother had scolded her, "A lady remains calm and gracious at all times." Bessie had never thought she would appreciate her rigid upbringing, but today she breathed a silent thank-you to her parents. With Mother's words stiffening her spine and strengthening her limbs, with William's eyes pleading and Robert tugging at her hand, Bessie stepped into the soddie.

For a moment, it was too dark to see, and she breathed in the damp earthy smell, reminiscent of an orchard after the leaves have fallen. Then, as her eyes adjusted to the dimness, she recoiled inside herself, stifling the urge to push at the ceiling, to push it away from her, keep it from crushing her.

"What will you need for the night?" William lifted the lantern toward her and she stared at the warm glow.

Keeping her voice low and calm, congratulating herself on how proud Mother would be, Bessie replied, "I just need my valise. Everything else can wait until morning."

The three of them stood almost shoulder to shoulder, then William shifted and put the lantern on the table. Three tin plates winked from the shelf along the wall. A cast iron frying pan stood on the tiniest stove Bessie had ever seen.

Where would they put their belongings? There was hardly room for three adults in this room. The bed with a dresser beside it, the table, four chairs, the tiny stove, and a narrow cupboard filled the place and there was no doorway to another room. This was it! Her new home!

The rattle of the harness came through the open door behind her, but all other noises had disappeared within the sod walls, except Robert's breathing. It filled the space.

She jerked to attention. He must be exhausted and here she

stood, worrying about where to put things. "Do you have your bag, Robert?"

"It's right here." His voice was lined with fatigue. "Shouldn't we put the boxes under shelter someplace?" He paused. "Just in case in rains."

"I can stack them at the foot of the bed." William offered, and ducking out the door, proceeded to carry them in one by one, the space shrinking with every box.

"I'll get a bucket of water for you." William lit another lantern and disappeared carrying a pail.

Grabbing Robert's hand, she turned to him. She knew her eyes were as large and dark as his but she couldn't be sure his expression wasn't a result of fatigue, unlike the fear that made her eyes feel wide.

"It will be fine," he assured her wearily. "We just need to get organized. I can keep my books in boxes at the end of the bed and we'll find some way to sort out the rest of our things. Maybe some hooks or. . ." His voice trailed wearily into silence.

She glanced around the dark, close room. *How can you hang hooks in dirt?* she thought, then saw that William's coat hung near the door. So it was possible.

There was no comfort in the thought. A bitter taste rose in the back of her throat. This room was no better than a small cave. A small, dark hole in a land of overwhelming space and brittle sunshine. It was surely a land of mocking extremes.

Oh for a cup of hot tea served in cool china! A plump chair. Warm carpeting under her feet. A window with more lighted windows from other nearby homes beyond.

She sucked in desperately but the air was too close, too earth-laden, and her head felt light. Shadows danced crazily.

I'll die, she thought. *I'll wither like a flower taken from the sun, fade like grass under a box. I'll suffocate, buried alive. I can't breathe.*

Robert coughed.

She filled her lungs and choked back the words rushing to her mind. Desperate, angry, burning words. Slowly, she let her breath out and regained control.

"How are you doing?" she asked him.

"Just tired," he sighed. "Let's go to bed. Things will look better in the morning. You'll see."

"I'm sure you're right," she murmured. Surely it was all a nightmare. She'd wake up in the morning and find it wasn't real.

෨

With the morning came harsh reality. A bar of sunshine blasted through a narrow window next to the table, barely relieving the gloom that shrouded the bed. Bessie clutched the quilt to her chin. It was the quilt she and Mother had made for William just before he moved west. "It has to be warm," Mother insisted. "We can't be certain what sort of quarters he'll have nor what the conditions will be." She'd filled it with double wool batts. Bessie remembered the warm brush of the rough wool pieces she'd stitched together for the patchwork top, and now she rubbed her fingertips across the warm pieces without opening her eyes.

The quilt was so warm and soft, the room so cold and bleak.

"Wake up, sleepy head," Robert teased and coughed. He sat up and coughed until his lungs loosened, then flung himself back on the bed, bouncing several times to see if she would respond.

"I'm awake," she growled. "Just not ready to get up." *If I keep my eyes closed maybe this dreadful place will disappear.*

"It's morning." He pulled a feather from the pillow and tickled her face.

She could feel the corners of her mouth twitch and familiarity stirred a sense of relief. As long as Robert was with her she could manage. There wasn't a day went by but he tried to add a bit of cheer. He did his best to ease life for her no matter how ill he was. The least she could do in return was to try and ease things for him.

He teased the feather over her nose again.

"Stop it!" She pulled the covers over her face, but he jerked them back down.

"Aren't you the cook around here?" He tickled her face.

She moaned and finally opened her eyes. How was she going to cook in this pit of gloom? All Mother's meticulous training meant nothing here.

"I'll have two eggs, some fried potatoes, and maybe fresh strawberry preserves." Robert smiled down at her.

"I think you'll have to find another cook then," she retorted and got a kiss for her cheekiness.

A thud on the door made them both jerk their heads up.

"Are you decent?" William's voice was muffled. "If you are, I'll start the fire."

"Come ahead," Robert called.

Robert and William discussed the weather, how well the trip had gone, the good night's rest they'd had, and how they would unpack the crates, but Bessie ignored them and stared unblinkingly at the roof over her. If one could call rough boards with sod drooping through the cracks a roof. She took a deep breath and closed her eyes. If she had been a praying person, she would have prayed for strength—and a sense of humor—but she had never been a praying person. She would have to find the strength within herself. Her training and her deep sense of duty would see her through this rough spot. It's only temporary, she reminded herself. She silently repeated the words several times before she was able to calm her unruly emotions and don a serene smile.

"I'm just going to do the chores," William called. "Twenty minutes of privacy and I'll be back." He pulled the door shut.

Bessie threw back the covers and swung her feet over the edge, reaching for her clothes. Then she remembered, and her feet hung poised in mid air. Dirt. She'd forgotten the floor was dirt. Holding back a moan, she found her stockings and shoes and pulled them on before she let her feet touch the floor.

"Where did William sleep?" she asked as she buttoned her dress.

"I'm not sure." Robert rolled out and stood behind her to pull on his trousers. Immediately he began to cough.

She hurried to the stove. William had filled the kettle and the water was already hot. She searched for tea leaves on the shelves and dumping a handful in the pot, waited barely long enough for the water to color, then stirred it vigorously. Robert's cough was loosening but she knew it would be a few minutes before this first morning spell would end. Hurrying back to his bag, she found the licorice root and added a pinch to the cup of tea.

Robert nodded gratefully when she handed him the steaming cup.

It wasn't until she returned from her trip to the outhouse that her question about where William slept was answered. A small lean-to had been built on one end of the soddie. She pushed open the door and shuddered. It was even smaller and darker than the main room. A rough bed covered with a horse blanket faced the door.

Guilt flooded Bessie. William hadn't uttered a word of complaint at having to share his cramped quarters with his sister and her husband. He had moved into this low room—surely intended as a storeroom—and given them his only covering.

She would remedy that before the day was out. They had brought supplies with them. Dishes, bedding, some food items, and, of course, books. Before they spent another night, she would somehow make things more comfortable. A blast of hot air greeted her when she opened the shanty, and she hurried to the stove to adjust the damper. After a careful search of the cupboards, she realized Robert's breakfast was going to be much simpler than the one he had ordered. Oatmeal with molasses to sweeten it was all she could offer. To her mental list of things to do today, she added, Bake bread.

They crowded around the small wooden table, Bessie purposely choosing the chair facing the window, needing the bright sunshine to drive the despair from her thoughts, despair that seemed to originate from the dark, earthen walls and roof surrounding her. She would not look at them. Instead, she studied the contents of the shelves in what she had dubbed the "kitchen area." A bag of navy beans, a red and white can of Magic baking powder, a tin of tea, salt and pepper, and a small sack of coffee beans next to the coffee mill. The dark, black walls.

She jerked her gaze to the table. Running her fingernail up and down a crack in the wood, she sipped her coffee then tightened her lips. Even the coffee tasted of dirt. She forced herself to listen to the men.

"If you get me a claw hammer or crow bar, I can open our crates and get everything organized," Robert said.

He'll soon have a place for everything and everything in its place. As if that would somehow insure that life made sense! It would for him. He had his books. He'd soon have a routine, and he had a purpose—to regain his health.

I have a purpose too, she reminded herself. *To take care of Robert so he'll get better quickly.*

If only she could find solace in books and a routine. She sucked in her stomach muscles and sat straighter. There was no need to let her surroundings influence her attitude. She could cope as well here as in a modern, light-filled kitchen.

Or so she told herself, but the thought did not loosen the knot at the base of her neck. Nor did it release the feeling of hopelessness that filled her.

"I'll give you a hand," William promised.

"William?" she began. There was one thing she could do and that was be an efficient housewife. No point in letting all her good training go to waste. "What about supplies?" She hurried on at the surprise in his face. "I don't see much on your shelves."

He relaxed. "I'll show you the storeroom after breakfast. I have flour there and a root cellar underneath. I grew a big potato garden last year. Still have potatoes even though I traded them all winter for meat and bread from the neighbors." He rose. "I'll help you with those crates," he said to Robert, and the two men went outside.

Bessie had washed the few dishes by the time they pried open the lids. Robert fell to his knees before the books as Bessie and William looked on.

"I might as well show you the storeroom," William nodded toward the door. Inside the lean-to, he pulled open a trap door and waved toward the ladder. "I think there's a turnip or two down there yet."

She stared at the hole in the ground, dread rippling along her spine. "Would you mind getting me a basin of potatoes?"

Chuckling, he said, "I'd forgotten your fear of spiders, or thought you'd outgrown it. Here." He handed her the lantern. "Hold this above the hole and I'll go down." From within the bowels of the earth, she heard the thud of vegetables filling the basin and then William's deep chuckle. "You should see this spider. Biggest one I ever saw. Big as a coat button."

She squealed. "Kill it. What if it crawls up here?"

William's head appeared in the opening.

"Did you kill it?"

He swung his legs over the edge and sat grinning at her. "What if she had babies? You want all her babies to be orphaned?"

"Yes, I do." She blew the light out and took the basin of potatoes. "I don't even like dead spiders," she muttered and hurried out the door. They stood side by side in the sunshine as she shook the basin, checking for any hiding bugs.

"How are you doing?" William asked, brushing a bit of dirt off the back of her hand.

She blinked as tears threatened, wondering how much he had guessed, for she knew he wasn't asking about spiders or supplies. William had always sensed her feelings better than anyone else in the family, and he understood. The others expected her to be calm and complacent. Any show of emotion was interpreted as a sign of wilfulness. William alone had allowed her space to sort things out.

She touched his arm and nodded. "I just want Robert to get better. I'll do whatever I can to help him."

He nodded and they returned to the soddie without saying anything more.

It was as if she had crossed a bridge, she thought later that morning, squatting beside her open trunk, as if she had been faced with a choice and decided which way to go. Not that she ever really had an option, but somehow, having made the commitment to do everything in her power to speed Robert's recovery, she felt like she had been involved in the direction her life took.

Absently, she lifted the hand-embroidered pillow slips from the trunk and stroked the bright flowers, delicately stitched by her own hands.

The only choice she had was her attitude, but fitting in cheerfully was one way she could make it possible for him to grow strong again.

She lifted her head and listened. A few minutes ago, Robert had finished arranging his books in packing crates stacked sideways like shelves, and gone outside, but she could not hear him. All she heard was the whistle of the meadowlark and the grass rustling in the wind. Briefly, she wondered where Robert had disappeared to, then shrugged and turned back to her task.

Carefully, she unwrapped the china cups and saucers, and the matching teapot, and set them on the shelf behind the table. They were a beacon of purity in this dirty hole. She lifted the rest of the linens, and from the bottom, withdrew the "Dresden Plate" quilt she and Mother had handstitched for months before her wedding. With its bright pieces on a pure white background, it was like a flag of home.

Hurrying to the bed, she stripped the dark wool quilt and grey flannel sheets and replaced them with the white linens she had brought. She slid the pillows into the hand-embroidered cases and was about to flip the Dresden Plate quilt on top when she paused. Slowly, she straightened and held the quilt up, stretching it over her head. It was as bright as a freshly painted wall; as colorful as the wallpaper in Mother's spare bedroom. She contemplated the idea. Why not? Why not hang it on the dirt wall behind the bed?

Grabbing up the bedding she'd removed, she hurried from the soddie.

"I should have known you'd find a book," she greeted Robert who sat tipped back in a chair against the sun-drenched wall.

He held the place in his book with a finger and lowered the chair to all fours. "I have never felt sun so warm," he murmured. "Makes me feel good to be alive." He looked at her. "What are you doing?"

"Just going to make William's bed now that we have our things unpacked." She ducked into the lean to and threw aside the horse blanket, rank with old sweat. Underneath was a bare gunny sack tick stuffed with straw. Punching it until it settled into what she hoped was a less lumpy bulk, she flipped the sheets over it and neatly made the bed. Stepping back out into the sunshine, she gasped for air, letting the sun drive away her shivers.

Settling herself on the ground next to Robert's chair, she stared at the stubby bunch of aspen guarding the outhouse. The leaves burst forth in lacy green, drinking up the sun's rays even as she was. Again, she felt the uncoiling of emotion. "'Wilfulness,'" her mother would say. *Uncertainty. Perhaps even fear,* Bessie argued silently. She leaned against Robert's leg and he dropped a hand to her shoulder, patting gently. Turning, she rubbed her cheek against his knee and looked into his face, letting the sight of his calm features touch her turmoil and diminish it.

He read a few more words then lifted his eyes to study her. "Are you feeling settled now?" he asked after a moment.

She wished she could tell him how unsettled she was feeling—as though she'd been transported to a foreign country. The soddie made her feel claustrophobic, and the endless sky made her feel lost. The wind moaned through her head until she wanted to cry, and she felt so alone. She knew he only wanted to know if she felt organized about her belongings. He had arranged his shaving kit and personal items in precision in the top two drawers of the dresser. His books and journal were as orderly as a library. She had hung her clothing from the hooks beside the bed and arranged the dishes and linens. "A place for everything and everything in its place," was his motto, his way of being settled.

"I think I've got things pretty well laid out," she answered. No point in unsettling his sense of well-being. He nodded and returned to his book. Leaning back against his leg, she let the sun soak her, wishing it would melt the icy crystals in her heart, but they remained untouched despite the warmth of the rays.

After a few drowsy moments, she gathered up her skirts and pushed herself to her feet. "I need you to help me with something."

Reluctantly, he lifted his head, loath to leave his book. "What?"

She hesitated, then rushed ahead. "I want to hang my quilt on the wall behind the bed and I need someone to help me tack it up."

His eyes clouded. "You want to put a quilt on the wall?"

"Yes." She nodded vigorously. "It will brighten the place."

He shrugged and she knew he didn't understand, but he got to his feet and set his book on the chair, stretching lazily. "What do you need?"

"I need a hammer and some tacks, I suppose." She hurried through the door. "See." Jumping up on the bed, she suspended the quilt across the wall. "It's like wallpaper. Doesn't it look better than dirt walls?"

He studied the quilt then looked at her, "I think you'll need to tack the quilt to a strip of wood and then nail that to the wall."

She flopped down on the bed, disappointment sharp. "How can I do that?"

"William showed me where he keeps his tools and material. I'll go see what I can find."

She was still seated on the bed—the quilt fanning out around her—when Robert returned.

"I found what we need," Robert's voice startled her. "And some gunny sacking to put behind it so it doesn't get soiled."

"There you go," he said a few minutes later as they stood back to admire the fresh wall covering.

"It looks so good!" She hugged herself.

He pulled her close. "I'm glad it makes you happy." He kissed her eyelids.

Yes, I will be happy. Every time I look at this wall, I'll remember to be happy. This will be my wall. The quilt is my banner to remind me we're only here for awhile. Just until Robert is better. I must keep in mind that life is more than this dark soddie and the vast empty sky.

three

"Bessie, look. I've found some more flowers," Robert called as he strode into the soddie.

Bessie carefully tipped the golden loaves of bread onto a clean tea cloth before she lifted her eyes to focus on the yellow bundle in his hand. "More flowers." It was neither question nor surprise. First, there had been the pale crocuses that swarmed with plant lice as soon as they warmed, then the frayed dandelions that withered in the dark soddie. Now these lemon snapdragon-like flowers. No one could accuse them of having any snap, she thought, for they were as alike as the navy beans filling the sack on the shelf.

"William calls them Buffalo Beans," Robert went on, eager in his enthusiasm. Stretching over the table, he grabbed a Mason jar from the shelf and filled it with water, then plunged the stems and brown roots into it.

Bessie bent over them to sniff.

"They're scentless," he informed her.

As had been the dandelions and crocuses before them. Everything in this country seemed to be deformed or underdeveloped. She stilled her resentful thoughts. Robert was already collecting his notebook and pencil from the packing-box shelf at the end of the bed. Never before had she seen him attempt sketching, but he seemed determined to learn all he could about the prairies and to record it.

"This country is full of odd and unusual things," he commented as he sat down at the table, studying the flowers with the intensity of a bee.

Flawed and unusable, she purposely twisted the words, but watching Robert bent over the page, she kept them safely inside her head. Already he had lost the deathly pallor that clung to him all winter. He now had a healthy-baby glow.

When he got brown and hardened, she would know he was ready to return to Toronto.

"Where is William?" Turning back to the stove, she lifted the lid off the soup pot, savoring the rich aroma of stewed meat and vegetables, as she stirred the mixture, thick with pot barley.

"He said he was going to start sowing his wheat today. He's sure pleased with moisture conditions. Says the ground is warm and fertile just waiting to give him a bumper crop. He wants to break thirty more acres this year."

Hearing the intensity in his voice, Bessie paused, her hand suspended above the soup. A large drop of rich brown juice beaded on the tip of the spoon and plopped into the pot. "I never thought to see him farming," she said. "I always think of him building things. There was that time he made a playhouse for me in the orchard back of the house." She paused. Come to think of it he had dug up wild daisies and put a row of them around the playhouse. "What he liked best was creating things with his hands: cupboards, shelves, and, later, houses."

"It's hard to believe they just give away a hundred and sixty acres. Just imagine. A whole quarter section of your own land."

"Yes. Just imagine!" He was too lost in his dreamy contemplation of free land to notice her sarcasm.

"Makes me wish for my own homestead."

"Robert!" She dropped the lid back on the pot with a clang and spun around to face him. Just talk of staying tipped her world and filled her with shards of fear. "You're a lawyer, not a farmer!"

"I know." His eyes held a faraway look unlike anything she had ever seen before. "But Mr. Scofield says land is a wise investment right now. He predicts the country will soon be settled up—a family on every quarter and flourishing towns and businesses."

Three days ago William had offered to take Robert with him when he went to finish a job in town. Robert had come back with an armload of books and filled with talk of local politics, but he had said nothing about this strange longing for land. She stared at him, unable to believe her ears, and then she let her gaze slip past him to the quilt hanging over the bed. Drawing in a slow breath, she held it inside her for a moment and let the memory of the day she'd hung the quilt over the cold dirt wall pull her back to calmness. She wouldn't argue with him, or let him know how much she hated this country. She had promised herself to do all she could to help him recover quickly and thoroughly. She let her breath out slowly, letting fear ride out on her warm breath.

"I thought you went to see Mr. Scofield to ask for some books to read."

"I did." He bent over his journal, sketching the buffalo beans. "We talked."

Talked? About owning land and staying here? She turned back to the stove, breathing deeply to still the warm flush that raced up her face—a warmth that had nothing to do with the hot stove. She shook her head. There was no way Robert could be seriously contemplating such a move. He belonged back east where he could build a successful practice.

No, she assured herself and took another deep steadying breath. *It's just his way. Always looking at things from every angle and assessing different options.* Probably he was making notes in his journal and had to list homesteading as one of the ways to survive on the prairies.

It should make an interesting topic. No wonder he thought about it. How did one survive month after month, year after year in these primitive, barbaric conditions? A shudder rippled across her shoulders. Thank goodness she wouldn't have to stay long enough to personally discover the answer.

"Smells mighty fine." William stomped his feet at the doorway. For an instant, he blocked the sunlight and then stepped over the sill. "Could a hungry man have something besides the smell?"

Bessie smiled at him. "It's ready." She sliced hot bread and filled bowls with soup. "Robert tells me you've begun planting."

"That I have." He beamed like he'd found a gold mine.

Bessie pursed her lips. Land seemed to have the same mysterious attraction gold did. "Gold fever" they called it. Was there also "land fever"?

"The land is rich as anything I've ever seen." He rubbed his hands together and grinned.

"No doubt you've seen a lot of land in your travels," she murmured, *being an experienced farmer and all.* It would be unseemly to voice the sarcasm she felt.

"Guess I have," he nodded. "Seen a bit as I crossed the country. Seen some to the north of here. Some was heavier than this but I don't remember any that had the same feel to it." He massaged his thumb along his fingers as if feeling the soil.

Jerking to her feet, she grabbed up the empty bowls and shoved them in the dishpan. "I'm going to walk to town today," she announced with a mouth that felt stiff. "Maybe there'll be mail from home." She emphasized "home," then whisked the crumbs off the table and faced them with arms crossed militantly across her chest. "Besides, the walk will do me good." *It will also do me good to find someone not so besotted with land as you two seem to be.*

"I have a letter ready to go to my mother," Robert said, barely glancing her direction before he turned back to William. "Tell me how you came to choose this particular piece of land."

❧

The door slapped shut behind Bessie. Her nose filled with lemon-oil and dill pickle smell as her eyes adjusted to the shadowed interior and she could focus on the bulging shelves, saws, and chains hanging from the rafters of the store. She saw someone who had to be Mr. Waley, with a thin, pinched face and wire-rimmed glasses perched on a large nose.

"Can I help you, ma'am?" His voice was reedy.

"Yes." She stepped toward the black wicket at the corner of the counter. "I've come for our mail. I'm Mrs. Macleod, William Wilson's sister," she rushed on as he raised his bushy black eyebrows.

His face settled into a smile. "Of course you are! William told us you and your husband were joining him." He sorted a bundle of letters. "Here're three letters for you." As she took them from him, he asked, "How are you folks doing?"

"Fine, thank you," she murmured as she glanced at the letters. One from her parents and another from a friend in Toronto. The third, from Ottawa, was addressed to Robert. His mother. She still didn't include Bessie in her correspondence, still thought Robert was her private property. Bessie sighed and tucked the letters into her basket and briskly turned back to Mr. Waley. "I'll just have a look around."

"You do just that." He moved away from the wicket. "If you need any help, you be sure and let me know."

She was putting a wedge of cheese in her basket when the screen door squeaked and she looked up. It was a tall young woman with a baby on her hip. A plump little girl clung to her skirts, and beyond the screen Bessie saw another child chasing a dog. She recognized the two children as the ones she had seen that first day.

"Come along now, Meg." The newcomer addressed the child at her skirts then noticing Bessie, rushed forward. "Welcome. You must be Mrs. Macleod. I've been awaiting your arrival ever since William told us you were coming." She held out her hand and clasped Bessie's. "I'm Margaret Pederson. We live just down the road at the edge of town."

Bessie's "How do you do? Pleased to meet you," barely interrupted the flow of chatter.

Glancing at Bessie's basket, Margaret raced on, "You about done here?" At Bessie's murmur of agreement, she continued, "Why then, you just come on over for tea." She bounced the baby on her hip and took the letter Mr. Waley pushed toward her. "I've been longing for someone to talk to. You can tell me all the news from back east. Come along now, Meg." She ushered the child through the door and Bessie hurried after them.

As the door squeaked open, a voice, sharp like a saw ripping through lumber, called from the room beyond the counter, "Who was that, Isaac? Isaac, you come back here this minute." The door slapped shut, cutting off the voice.

Margaret giggled. "That was Mrs. Waley. Did you see her?"

"I didn't know she was there until just now." Bessie turned to stare at the closed door briefly before following Margaret down the street.

Margaret's blue eyes twinkled. "No one's ever seen her, but I bet she knows everything that goes on in that store. Poor Mr. Waley." She laughed. "I wonder why his mother hides. Sometimes I make up all kinds of reasons." Without pausing, she called, "Billy, come along home."

Suddenly Bessie laughed, a tickle from deep within her stomach. "Poor Mrs. Waley. Maybe she's shy."

Margaret grinned. "Doesn't matter. Gives me something to think about." She glanced around her as she unhooked the gate keeping back the chickens. "Not much else to amuse myself with." She stepped aside and let Bessie and the children through before pulling the gate shut and latching it. "There aren't many women-folk around here. And few of them has time to visit."

Bessie stared down the street. A man drove a wagon toward the livery barn. The sun glistened off the narrow building next to Mr. Scofield's office. "What about Millie's Ladies Fashions?" She read the name from the window.

"Millie's nice, I guess. Awfully old and awfully busy. I think she used to be a preacher's wife or something." Margaret bounced the baby up on her hip and opened the door. "Come on in." She dropped a blanket on the floor and set the baby on it. Straightening, she waved Bessie into the room. "Come on in and set. I'll put the kettle on."

Bessie stood in the doorway and stared. Frothy curtains at the windows, a small oak table with a glistening lace cloth, a stiff horsehair chesterfield and a small wooden rocker padded with dark green cushions. She couldn't take her eyes from the rocker. How she missed having a comfortable chair.

She moved to it, running her hands across the golden wood of the arms, rocking it gently with her fingertips. It whispered as it swayed. She settled into the chair, and closed her eyes as she rocked and rocked. There was consolation in the swaying motion.

"I'm sorry I took so long," Margaret bustled in carrying a tea tray with two white china cups and a brown china teapot. Never had a plain brown teapot looked so good. It was a reminder of home and better times. She had forgotten the satisfaction of simple routines and ordinary activities. A wave of reassurance washed through her, and she smiled.

Somehow she would inject a bit of civilized routine into life at the soddie. She wasn't sure how, and she knew it wouldn't be the same as here in this bright home, but somehow she would do it.

"I had to see that Billy and Meg were playing before I left them. They're quite a pair. I suppose it must be their age but it seems they can find more things to get into than enough. Yesterday they took it upon themselves to feed the chickens. Dumped a whole bag of wheat on the ground before I caught them. I had to clean up as much as I could so it wouldn't be wasted. You take sugar or milk in your tea?"

"No thanks." Bessie took the cup from Margaret, smiling her appreciation.

"Now you take my little Benny here." Margaret beamed at the little boy at her feet. The child smiled around the two fingers in his mouth. "This one just sits wherever I plop him." She sighed and brushed a strand of blond hair off her forehead. "Trouble is, it won't last much longer." As she spoke, the baby rocked back and forth on his bottom, reaching for a block just out of his reach. "I do rattle on, don't I? So tell me, how do you like it out here?"

Bessie set her cup down and tried to collect her thoughts. "I. . .I think it is going to be good for my husband."

Margaret nodded. "William said he hasn't been well. Lung trouble?"

Nodding, Bessie explained, "He's had weak lungs all his life. The air out here is supposed to help."

"I surely hope it does. It must be an awful worry for you."

Bessie met her eyes and swallowed. No one, not even her mother had ever acknowledged that Robert's ill health was cause for Bessie to worry. They simply expected her to do her duty. "I try to make the best of it." Her voice whispered softly. "Hopefully I can make life comfortable for him and speed his recovery."

Margaret studied her with narrowed eyes and had opened her mouth to comment when Benny started to fuss. His mother scooped him up and allowed him to nurse.

"Are you getting settled right well?" Margaret asked as the baby quieted down.

"As best I can. It's smaller than I had imagined."

Margaret laughed merrily. "I've seen a few of those shanties built by bachelors. They have all the appeal of a jail cell. Just the bare necessities, thank you. No need for any niceties." Her eyes twinkled. "My guess is William's place isn't any better despite the fact he's a nice man."

Bessie laughed, feeling some of the tightness in her chest relax. "It's pretty simple." *And dark, and gloomy, and depressing.*

Margaret looked at her intently. "I always think soddies are so dim and small. I don't know if I could stand to live in one. What's it really like?"

Bessie tried to look away, but the compassion and understanding in Margaret's eyes held her. Here was someone who understood, but Bessie could not confess her dark, angry feelings, not even to someone whose eyes were filled with sympathy. Nodding slowly, she simply said, "It's workable. Robert is already showing improvement. Maybe. . .if he is better by fall . . .maybe we'll. . ." She couldn't finish. She didn't dare think of the alternatives. Stay in the soddie for the winter! It didn't bear contemplation. Surely it wouldn't be healthy for Robert's lungs.

Margaret patted her hand. "I'm sure everything will work out." A piercing wail came from the yard. Margaret sighed. "I better see what it is. Do you mind holding the baby?" She placed the drowsy child in Bessie's arms.

Baby Benny's eyes widened for an instant and he touched Bessie's cheek with his warm, plump hand and then his eyelids dropped and he cuddled into her arms.

Bessie studied the sleeping little one. How she longed to have a child of her own. With Robert's illness and this trip west, perhaps it was for the best that she had not yet conceived. She stroked the baby's cheek and smiled as he made sucking sounds. *Maybe by this time next year.* . .She let her thoughts drift to promises of home, a baby, Robert well again.

four

The visit with Margaret improved Bessie's spirits. Margaret's non-stop chatter and almost irreverent sense of humor had refreshed her. At the same time, she had learned a lot about the community, things she knew William would never have told her, nor Robert if he heard them from Mr. Scofield. Bessie laughed as she recalled Margaret's imitation of the fuss Mrs. Bliss made when Mr. Waley read aloud the return address on her mail. Of course, she and Margaret discussed informative things as well. Bessie knew that Mrs. Niels just north of town acted as the midwife and could be counted on for medicinal advice. Margaret also told Bessie of the plans to construct a school building in the fall. This was especially important to Margaret with Billy already five years old and Meg just eighteen months younger.

This, she acknowledged, she might have eventually heard from either William or Robert, but it was infinitely more satisfying to discuss it with Margaret.

Margaret also told her of the community picnic planned for Victoria Day. Everyone would take time away from their farm work even if the seeding wasn't completed. It was too great an event to miss. She said there would be races and games for the children. The men looked forward to horse-shoes and baseball, but if Margaret wasn't mistaken, the women cared more about getting together and visiting than any of the planned events.

As Bessie returned home, the sun was bright in the afternoon sky, making brittle shadows across the twin paths of the trail. Occasionally, a handful of clouds crossed the sun and softened the shadows. For a minute, she would feel the chill of the wind and pull her shawl around her shoulders, but the chill passed as quickly as it came. Across the unbroken

34

prairie, the pale blue of the crocuses had given way to waving silver fringes. The stunted trees were now fully leafed out, and beneath the dry yellow blanket of last year's prairie wool she could see a fresh green carpet of new grass.

She should have been happy as she walked along the rutted trail. She should have revelled in the purity of nature and in the wonder of a new-found friend, for she hadn't forgotten her wish that the lady behind the picket fence would be close to her age and someone she could feel some kindredship with. Her wish had been granted but her mind was a whirl of accusing thoughts.

A woman's duty is to serve her husband's needs.

She stood dirt still, holding her breath, not daring to turn around. It was as if her mother were standing behind her saying those words, and for a minute it alarmed her. She shook her head. It was just her imagination, she assured herself, and taking a deep breath, started walking again.

How often Mother had used the word duty as she trained Bessie. It was her duty to learn to cook a good meal, set a fine table, organize a quiet home, tend the children when she had some.

It was her duty to be quiet and peaceable and to avoid arguments.

It was her duty. . .

Duty seemed to cover every aspect of her life.

Not that she meant to be rebellious. She loved Robert. He understood her and, understanding, offered encouragement, not criticism. He was gentle and kind, and she was so proud of him. If only he would hurry and get better.

No, she surely didn't want to be rebellious, or troublesome, or whatever name her mother would have given if Bessie had confessed how her heart seemed so full of empty corners. Nor could she explain those empty corners to anyone—let alone her mother. She failed to understand them herself.

She had everything she had dreamed of and wanted, a fine husband and a promising future waiting for them. There was no reason to complain. Yet, an angry blackness filled her mind, a blackness filled with the dank oppressive smell of a cellar, a darkness barely relieved by the bar of light through a small window. The airlessness of the soddie seemed to close around her heart, squeezing her chest until she could barely breathe. All the vague, restless feelings in her heart were harnessed in that one thing: the soddie.

A pile of white clouds passed over the sun and she clutched her shawl. The clouds were like soap suds whipped up in fresh hot water, reminding her of her first wash day on the prairie. When she'd asked William how she was to manage the task, he had said it was simple.

"It's easy in the warm weather. You have the whole outdoors to work in." As he spoke, he lifted a copper boiler to the top of the minuscule stove and filled it with water. It was to stay there all night heating. All night Bessie and Robert roasted in their bed like two loaves of bread.

It crossed her mind to ask how a person did the wash during the winter months, but it didn't concern her enough to question her brother. What a mercy, they'd be gone by then.

The parcel of groceries was growing heavy and Bessie's steps had begun to lag. Setting the parcel on the ground, she settled down on the rough grass to rest, though in truth, she confessed to herself, she was simply finding ways to delay her return to the soddie.

What's the matter with me? She was young and strong and could deal with this inconvenience for a few weeks until Robert got his strength back. She would think of it as an adventure and be forever grateful that it was temporary.

Having done her best to cheer herself up, she struggled to her feet and resumed her journey homeward.

❧

She was stirring oatmeal for breakfast when William burst through the door, a chill racing across the floor in his wake.

"I just made it." He set the bucket of milk on the table and reached his hands toward the stove, rubbing them together. "We're about to be dumped on."

"It's going to rain?" Robert looked up from the table where

he was sipping his morning cup of tea. Bessie watched him set the cup down and noted that he didn't cough. Unaware that she had been doing so, and without looking directly at him, she discovered with some amusement, she had been observing him all morning, measuring how much he coughed and how many sips he needed before he could breathe easier. She was happy to see that there had been an improvement over the last month.

William grinned and turned to Robert. "It looks like it's settling in to give us a soaker."

The sound of him rubbing his palms together grated on her nerves. She missed the morning shaft of sunshine that normally brightened the corner by the stove. All she got today was a weak grey wash of light that did little to relieve the gloom of the room or the despair that continued to dog her days.

Keeping her back to her brother and husband as they rejoiced over the perfect timing of the impending rain, she scolded herself for her selfishness. She knew she should be happy for William. Several times lately he had commented that the fields, bursting with the green of his emerging wheat crop, were in need of a rain, but all she could think was that it meant being confined to the soddie today with barely enough light to drive the darkness into its customary corners.

"It's started already," William reported from his post before the narrow window. Wind-driven rain slashed across the landscape.

Robert joined William. "Well, I'll be! The rain is actually falling sideways. I've never seen anything like it."

William's deep chuckle filled the room. "The power of the prairie wind."

Bessie had observed him more than once turning his face toward the sun and taking off his hat to let the wind tear at his scalp. Every time she wondered how he could enjoy the ceaseless wind. She hated it. It grabbed her skirts and hair. It flung dust into her eyes. Moaning and shrieking like a demented woman, it shredded her nerves.

As she turned to set the table, a drop of blackish water

plopped on the table. "Oh no!" she moaned and grabbed an empty bowl. "The roof is dripping."

"Best get ready," William warned. "Out here we say for every day of rain outside, we get three inside." He chuckled as he grabbed a pot to catch a drip next to the window.

How can he laugh? she fumed as she checked the roof for further leaks. Robert, at least, seemed to share some of her anxiety. He stood in front of the packing cases that had become his book shelves holding a cup in each hand, ready to prevent any damage to his beloved friends. She was about to turn her attention back to breakfast preparations when she saw a black trail seep down the center of her Dresden Plate quilt.

"No!" She hadn't meant to shriek, but didn't pause to apologize. Grabbing the dishpan, she leaped onto the bed, unmindful of the mud clinging to her shoes. Lifting the pan to the ceiling, she tried to catch the drip, but it seeped through next to the wall and her efforts were in vain.

She couldn't let it get any worse. Jumping from the bed, she grabbed the dishtowel from the back of a chair, and using a table knife jabbed the cloth into the oozing ceiling then leaned back, watching as the towel grew dark with mud-laden seepage. A drip formed and plopped into the basin at her feet and she sighed. At least it wasn't dripping on her beautiful quilt.

Slowly, half fearing what she would see, she lifted her gaze to the quilt. A stain ran down the center of it like a ragged tear. In several places the dirty water had bled into the bright handstitched pieces.

"It's ruined," she whispered, not daring to face the men though acutely aware of their silence in a room full of the sound of water dripping into tin containers.

"Bess?" Robert's voice was pleading and gentle. "Maybe, you'll be able to wash it out."

She shook her head. "No. It's ruined. I'll never get the stain out." Nevertheless, she pulled a clean rag from her pile and dampening it with warm water, began to dab at the ugly mark, managing to remove some mud. The rest of the unsightly stain, she knew, was permanent.

William cleared his throat and she met his eyes. It was as it had always been between them. She knew he understood the quilt meant a lot to her, and he was sorry, but he would never come right out and say it. His unspoken sympathy touched her bruised heart and she blinked back tears determined to prove she was no longer a little girl who cried at every disappointment.

"I'm sorry," Robert murmured, grabbing her hand to pull her toward him. For a moment she rested her face against his shoulder and as he rubbed her back some of her hurt eased. Then at the sound of a new drip, Robert shifted, reaching toward the shelves to catch it before it harmed his books.

Bessie straightened and smoothed her hair. Drawing a deep breath, she stilled her emotions. It wasn't anyone's fault. It was just the way things were out here. She knew she couldn't expect them to understand this quilt hanging against the black walls of the soddie was more than a decoration, a piece of handiwork, or even a reminder of home. It was her slice of sanity in a world that seemed to have tilted on its axis. It was her assurance that things would return to normal.

Now its perfection was flawed. Its promise was no longer bright.

"I've been meaning to tell you my plans," William broke the noisy silence. The deepening of his voice warned her he was about to say something important and her heart tightened with fear. Despite hating the soddie, she had worked out a routine that allowed her a certain sense of purpose and control.

She dared not think what she would do—what they would do—if this were ripped from them.

"I'm going to build a house."

Robert and Bessie looked at each other for a moment and she could see he was as surprised and troubled as she.

"I received a message yesterday that my lumber had arrived at the railhead. I was planning to pick it up." He glanced out the window and ruefully shook his head. "But it will have to wait until the weather clears."

She looked from one man to the other, filled with disquieting thoughts. They were already beholden to William for his hospitality. Even though his home was barely big enough for one person, let alone three, he'd never uttered one word of complaint. Now this. He would end up resenting them for intruding into his life.

She knew by the white spot in Robert's forehead, right above his nose, that he was having similarly anxious thoughts. He unconsciously rubbed the spot as if it bothered him. Slowly, in his precise way, Robert asked, "It's not because of us, is it?"

His question startled William. Bessie guessed by the way he frowned that he didn't understood their concern. "Of course not," he assured them. "This soddie was only meant to be temporary, until I had time to build my own place. I want a good house—one I could bring a wife to."

Bessie and Robert nodded, Bessie letting herself breathe again, relieved he had planned a new home before they came. She was happy to know he hadn't put a halt to his own personal plans because of their presence.

"I think it sounds wonderful," Robert agreed. "So long as you remember that we are only here for a short time, so don't change any of your plans on our account."

"Agreed." The two men shook hands.

Bessie enjoyed seeing the closeness that had developed between them in such a short time. As they discussed the proposed building, she returned to fixing breakfast and to her own thoughts. She heard William say he hoped to have the house completed by fall but, apart from being glad for him, felt it would make little difference to her. By fall, they would be gone. Quickly counting on her fingers, she named the months. *This is May. June, July, August, September. Four months—five at the most.*

If she could survive that long! By then she might have turned into a shrieking maniac whose cries matched those of the endless wind. In five months, she would lose her mind living in this cellar. She knew she would. Margaret had told her lots of stories about women who had run into the empty prairie and simply disappeared. Or worse, they had let their mind vacate their body and sat silently staring into space. She remembered how Margaret's voice dropped to a whisper as she talked about the worst cases of all, the ones who had grown violent and shrill. One woman had actually burned her husband and children to death.

Shuddering, she jerked her thoughts to a halt, alarmed at the direction they had taken, and tried to dismiss the dreadful weight that settled around her.

She wouldn't let it happen to her. She would hold on to the promise of home, but between her and the fulfilment of that promise was a black empty hole filled with fears and angry despair. She'd tried. She'd tried so hard, determined to make the best of it, to do her duty and thus speed Robert's recovery. She made thick rich soups, nourishing puddings, and mounds of mashed potatoes. She'd smiled and hummed and held her coiling emotions at bay, but she couldn't shake the feeling that the soddie grew steadily smaller every day. The roof was falling in on her. Every night she spread the covers and held the lantern high as she carefully checked for spiders. Nor could she lay her head on the pillow until she had shaken it so vigorously that surely any lurking bug would have been flung to his death. Yet she fell asleep every night with her skin crawling as she imagined spiders swarming up the walls, over the covers and across her face and legs.

She swallowed back the terror that raced up her throat and forced herself to concentrate on stirring the porridge, but her hand stirred without her mind changing direction. It remained engaged in battle with her fears.

There was no safe place from the eight-legged creepy intruders, she discovered. After the first day, when she nearly died of fright at the sight of a spider racing up the side of the saucepan, she never lifted anything from the self without first peering into it.

Filling three bowls with the steaming oatmeal and pouring coffee into the mugs, she announced, "Breakfast is ready," surprised at how calm her voice was. Only she knew of the tightness in her throat.

The one thing that gave her satisfaction was the way Robert ate. She had never known him to have a robust appetite, but in the month they'd been here, she had seen a steady increase in the amount he ate and the eagerness with which he welcomed food. The hollows in his cheeks were almost gone.

She smiled and pushed aside her turmoil as she so often had these past weeks. The strange thing was, the more she pushed away the emptiness inside her, the more hungry it grew. She was sure it would someday swallow her if she didn't find a way to satisfy it, but she knew not how to fill it! With difficulty she swallowed a desperate wail, forcing it back to the pit of her stomach, willing it to stay buried and hidden.

By next morning, the rain had quit—at least outdoors, but William was right. Inside it continued to drip in an irregular rhythm of splash and ding, dirty spots staining almost every surface; cups, jars and pots filling with murky water. While the sun shone brightly outside, inside the room was cold and clammy, the walls beginning to steam as the day grew warmer.

Bessie had just finished the breakfast dishes, her hands moving with forgetful slowness when Robert came to the door.

"Come on outside and enjoy the sunshine. It's lovely and warm out here. Leave the door open and give this place a chance to dry out."

Bessie nodded wearily. "I can do some mending." Gingerly she pulled the darning basket from under the bed carrying it at arm's length through the door to deposit it on the ground. She kicked it, jumping back, waiting for any nesting spiders to escape. None appeared and she retrieved a knitting needle to poke at the balls of yarn and rolled up socks, jumping back quickly after each jab.

Robert chuckled. "Here, let me check." He picked up the basket and stirred the contents with his hand while Bessie shuddered in horror.

"It's safe." His voice was low and teasing as he handed the

basket to her.

Keeping her hands behind her back, she kept her eyes on the yarn. "You didn't look on the very bottom."

He held the basket toward her. Slowly, she raised her eyes, and seeing the tenderness in his expression managed a wan smile.

"Please be sure," she said.

"You're right. There might be a spider still lurking in here." He grabbed the socks and yarn in his hand, and turning the basket over, knocked it against his leg. Then he made a great show of stomping the ground, but Bessie had seen the spider drop beside his boot and knew it wasn't just for show.

She shuddered as he returned the contents and handed the basket to her. "Thank you," she whispered, forcing herself not to shiver as she sat on the chair Robert placed for her in the sunshine. She pulled out one of William's socks. At least she could help repay his kindness by repairing his clothing while she was here.

Robert stood beside her, rocking back and forth on his heels, his hands on his hips.

"Smell the air," he said, and filled his lungs greedily. "It's so fresh after the rain."

She threaded the yarn through the needle and pulled the heel of William's sock tightly over the darning ball. The only good thing about the air, she thought, was that it wasn't raining any more. It was warm, too. She still felt damp from the conditions indoors.

However, as the doctor predicted, the Alberta air did seem to contain some mysterious healing quality. For the first time since she'd met him, and at his own admission, since he could remember, Robert had a vigorousness that made him seem years younger.

"Feel the sun." He stretched upward as he spoke.

He almost worshiped the sun, she thought. Well, she couldn't blame him. It had restored color to his face and it warmed him to the bones, as he insisted on saying.

"The sky is so blue. Have you ever seen anything like it?"

She didn't bother to look up from her task. There was a heaviness around her heart that prevented her from responding to the offerings of nature. She felt like she had sunk to the bottom of a pit. Listening to the drip, drip, plunk of leaks all night, coping with the dampness and the musty smell, and most of all seeing her beautiful quilt soiled had acted like a flood in her soul. A flood of dirty, smelly water in which she was drowning—not physically, of course, but inside. Something inside just seemed to wither up and die, or drown, or disappear into a vacuum.

It seemed like more than she could do to hold her head up, to keep her eyes open and focused on the task before her. To stir up an enthusiastic response to the beauties of the outdoors, especially in this unwelcoming land—well, she didn't have enough energy to even think about it.

"I'm going for a walk," Robert announced, but he didn't step away. Instead he grasped her shoulder and leaned over to kiss her cheek. He smelled of soap and licorice and she noticed how strong his lips felt against her skin. There was a stirring low in her stomach. For a moment his hand lingered on her shoulder and then he spoke close to her ear, his voice low and measured.

"Bessie, I'm proud of the way you're managing in these circumstances. We'll be fine, I promise you." Then he straightened and with a pat on her arm said, "Enjoy the sunshine." With that he strode across the yard.

She stared after him, tears blurring her vision. No wonder she loved him so much. He was so enamored of the sun and sky and the openness of the prairie that she was sure he had no idea how the soddie depressed her, nor how the space frightened her. Yet he understood that it was difficult for her and let her know he was concerned.

For a moment, she considered running after him and taking his hand. It had been so long since they had walked together hand in hand, since before they came out west for the "'cure." But already he had crossed the yard and was on the pathway bordering the wheat field. His stride was long and vigorous—

that of a healthy confident man. Her heart swelled with pride. He had such a regal bearing. Even when he was sick and almost too weak to walk, he had carried himself tall and upright, his head always lifted high as he studied his surroundings with avid interest. He was such a gentle, kind man.

Her throat clogged with tears and she wiped her hands across her eyes. She knew she was fortunate to have a good man. She was grateful he was regaining his strength. As she watched him, she mentally measured his progress. The first week out here, he had barely been able to make it across the yard, but it wasn't long before he created his own path across the end of the wheat field. Then he had gone to the little bluff of trees beyond the field. Today she prayed, let him make it to the rock pile William had made at the corner of the field.

Today the rock pile.

Tomorrow, the top of the hill.

Then home again.

five

The summer dragged on—hot, dusty and riddled with flies; measured, for Bessie, not in days or hours, but by the distance Robert walked each day and how often he coughed. Daily he improved, and she counted the lengthening distance between coughing spells, knowing assuredly that Robert was getting better. He would soon be well enough to travel. It was only a matter of time, she reassured herself many times a day, soothing her churning emotions with that promise.

The sameness of the daily routine frustrated her, but gave her reason to thank her mother for the proper training she'd given her. It was this training that enabled her to go about her duties, planning and conducting the household affairs smoothly. Determined to repay William's generosity, she had made preserves from the early pie plant, and later, from the wild saskatoons berries that grew in the deep coulees of the prairie.

The monotony of her daily routine was overlaid with the more important task of waiting, of counting and measuring Robert's recovery. It consumed her thoughts and helped her remain cheerful. Apart from the weekly trips to Ryanville, which combined shopping and the soul-satisfying visits with Margaret, the single interruption to the unending routine was the community picnic on May twenty-fourth, and the relief it provided was quickly forgotten.

Normally, it was Bessie who stopped to see Margaret on her trips to town, but one sun-laden day Margaret, her husband, Tom, and the children arrived unannounced on the doorstep with a bulging picnic basket.

"It's a grand and glorious day," Margaret announced. "Come and join us for a picnic. You, too," she called to Robert where he sat with his chair tipped against the sunny side of the soddie.

46

He dropped his chair to all four legs, carefully closing his book and putting away his pen before he turned to Bessie. "Bessie?"

She readily agreed. Nothing could have pleased her more than to get away from the soddie and spend the day in the company of Margaret and her family. The men already knew each other well enough to be comfortable visiting so they could be counted on to amuse each other.

"I have a favorite spot I could show you," Robert offered to Bessie's surprise. She knew he was spending more and more time walking but thought his only goal was to regain his strength. It hadn't occurred to her that he might find cause for enjoyment in his daily journey. Though, on second thought, it shouldn't surprise her. Robert was always exploring. From the beginning, he had attempted to identify as much of the flora and fauna of the area as he could. He was a confirmed note maker.

Robert and Tom led the way past the wheat field with stalks now bent with grain, past the rock pile almost hidden behind the tall grass, past the rustling poplar trees, and around a little knoll to a narrow path up the side of a hill. Bessie was pleased to see Robert able to keep pace with Tom's stride. Inside her, a golden warmth glowed. He was better. The country had done him good. Her waiting was almost over. Her thoughts raced ahead to the future. It wouldn't take them long to pack their few belongings. At the thought of the tiresome return journey, she almost wilted, but they could endure it because of what lay ahead.

Home. Not knowing when they would need it again, they had let their charming little house go, but they would find another place to live as soon as possible. She felt a pang of regret that someone else was living in the house they had first shared, but it had seemed the wisest thing to do at the time.

The memory of those wretched winter months and the almost forgotten terror of not knowing if Robert would live to share a home with her caught her so sharply she stumbled, but she managed to catch herself before Margaret noticed. Robert had been that close to death, and even now she couldn't bear to think about it. What a mercy it was all in the past.

"Bessie, you've got to see this." Robert was waiting at the crest of the hill, and taking her hand, pulled her forward. With one arm around her shoulders, he turned her to face the view. "Would you look at that!" His voice was low and so full of marvel that rather than look at the scene as he was urging her, she turned and looked into his face. Robert rarely enthused about anything, but his eyes glowed as he gazed at the land before him. Slowly, almost fearfully because of the effect on her husband, Bessie turned to see what held his attention so raptly.

Before her, the land fell away in soft waves to a distant smoky horizon. It was vast and open as if seen from the height of heaven. Bessie couldn't move or speak. She felt her jaw go slack.

"I've been here a hundred times or more but I never get tired of seeing it." Robert's voice was low and hushed. "It's like you can see forever."

Tom and Margaret had joined them and stood arm in arm drinking in the view with sighs of appreciation.

"There's the big barn Johnson put up." Tom pointed. "Why that must be twenty miles from here."

"I had no idea there was a country like this." Robert said. "A place where the beauty is in details—like tiny flowers, patterns in the grass, shapes in the wind. Where the weather and the colors can change in just a matter of hours, and the air and the sun are so pure."

Bessie twisted about so she could watch him. What had come over him? He seemed to have shed his normal reserve like a dry layer blown away by the wind. Nor was it his courtroom manner with which he quietly, but firmly and distinctly, expressed his opinion. This was different. He was so intense, yet he seemed so full of gentle peace. It was as if the vast space before them had some hypnotic power. Uneasiness rippled through her and nervously, she stepped away from the edge.

"You wait 'til you live through a prairie winter before you say how great it is," Tom warned him. "Now that's what proves if you're a man or not."

Robert smiled gently. "William's told me stories about it. Sounds like a real challenge." His eyes sought the horizon again and lingered there. He seemed to drink in the view like a man who has found water after a desert crossing. "It's just that I know it's a place where a man knows who he is and can be happy."

Her heart kicked against her ribs and she gasped for breath. Surely, he was talking in generalizations, not personally. After all, there was a future waiting for them back home. Her father had promised to keep a position open in his law firm for Robert's return. She looked out at the scene, but her eyes did not see the view, nor even the horizon. She sought the unseen; the security and shelter of home.

Margaret called her away, and the rest of the afternoon passed pleasantly enough. Despite the joy of playing with the children, hugging affectionate little Benny, and talking with Margaret, however, the disquieting feelings did not leave. She couldn't share her fears with Margaret. Not when they were so hazy.

❧

Bessie poured the dishwater out on the ground. Straightening, she looked around. Summer was losing its hold on the land. Already the wheat had turned to gold, rippling in hypnotic waves while bright yellow leaves flashed in the aspen groves. Shielding her eyes from the brightness of the shimmering sky, Bessie turned to search for Robert and saw him striding across the yellowed prairie, his steps long and forceful, his arms swinging at his side. She didn't need to see his face to know that it had grown golden brown. He had shed the pallor of his illness and developed a youthful zest. He was well—at his own confession, better than he'd ever been.

Tilting the basin against the wall, Bessie hurried out to meet him, ripples of anticipation filling her heart. Nothing had been said about travel plans and she had grown tired of waiting, every day expecting Robert to say it was time, every day feeling the thud of disappointment when they fell asleep without any mention of it. Today she was going to ask him to set a date.

Robert's whistling stopped as she met him beside the wheat field. "Ah, Bessie, isn't it a marvellous day?"

Thinking today she would begin to prepare for the return trip, she readily agreed. "Alberta has been good for you, better than the doctor hoped."

Robert nodded, his attention on the undulating field of grain. "Look at the bounty of this crop. This land will attract people from all over. It's a country with unlimited potential."

"I'm glad William has found such a nice spot," she said, but she was only peripherally concerned with William's good fortune.

"It's a land full of miracles. Especially for me. I've never felt better in my life." Robert put his arm around her shoulder and pulled her close. Wrapping her arms about his waist she looked up into his face.

"It's wonderful to see you looking so well." Her heart overflowed with gratitude. Robert looked younger than she'd ever seen him. He had an eagerness about him as if he wasn't sure how to restrain the energy flowing through his veins and fleshing out his bones. Despite her own difficulty in living in the soddie and dealing with her restlessness, she could never hate this land. It had restored her husband to her. For that she would be forever grateful.

Now they could return home. Her heart swelled with happiness.

"You're certainly well enough to travel." She cradled his face in her hands. Even his skin felt different. Warm and firm.

Robert took her hands in his own. "Where would you propose we go?" he teased.

Confused by his words, she studied his expression. "Why home of course."

"By home, I assume you mean Toronto?" His face sobered. She pulled her hands away, a vague stirring in her stomach making her uneasy. "Of course I mean Toronto. What other home do we have?"

"Bess, come here." Taking her by the hand, he drew her toward a large rock and urged her to sit. He stood facing her, leaning forward intently. "Bessie, I have always been sick. I expected to struggle with ill health all my life, but look at me. I have never felt better. I can walk and run without coughing or even struggling for breath. It's almost too good to be true. It's as the doctor said. This dry Alberta air has healed my lungs. If I go back east, my trouble may well start again."

Panic-driven nausea rose in Bessie's stomach and she swallowed hard to keep from vomiting. Her eyes refused to focus. She could have been staring at a stranger. Indeed, he was a stranger. This was not the Robert she had married. The Robert she knew had no secret yearnings to be an adventurer. A pioneer.

"I wish there was some way to make this easier for you." He spread his palms imploringly. "I don't want to go back."

Bessie opened her mouth, but no words came out. She swallowed hard and tried again. "But we never intended to stay." Her voice cracked and she sucked the inside of her mouth trying to moisten her dry tongue. "It was only until you got better, and you're better now. You're strong enough to travel." Her words were stiff and broken.

"Everything you say is true, but what if returning means my health troubles come back? I can't take that risk." He paused and searched her face intently. "Can you?"

It wasn't fair of him to ask, Bessie fumed. As if he could twist the truth and make her responsible. Lawyers! Sometimes their logic skipped a cog, yet there was no arguing with them. They could always twist your words to make them say something you didn't intend.

"You promised," she whispered. "You promised we'd only stay until you were better. Everybody promised." She sounded like a disappointed child, but she didn't care. Everybody had promised. "Just until he's better. It won't be for long." Her mother had said it, her father, even Robert's mother had said it. Though from Mrs. Macleod's lips, it had sounded more like an order than words of encouragement.

Well, he is better! She wanted to scream the words to a world she was afraid wouldn't listen.

Robert broke into her thoughts, his voice low. "I never promised, but I admit we both assumed this would be temporary."

"You still have a job with my father." Her voice grew stronger as she spoke. "Out here you have no job. We can't stay." The last words rang with triumph.

"I've been making plans."

"Plans?" He'd never said anything. Her mind twisted so violently she felt sick again and she lowered her head forcing herself to take slow deep breaths. If she threw up, this conversation would be over before she could make Robert see the folly of staying, and she swallowed back the bitter taste in her mouth.

Robert nodded and went on slowly. "Mr. Scofield has been wanting a partner. I'm going to open a law practice in his office."

He had said something about Mr. Scofield's desire to expand his business, but she thought it was only conversation, like the news she shared after visiting Margaret. She'd never dreamed Robert had been considering it.

She shook her head, trying to clear it so she could think. All summer she had clung to the promise of going home. It had been her lifeline. Now he was threatening to take it from her. There had to be something she could say to convince him to keep his promise, but all she could think of was, "We can't stay. We just can't." She looked around wildly. "Where would we live?"

Robert's eyes widened and she knew he hadn't even thought about it. "We could stay where we are, I suppose, if William is agreeable."

At her cry of protest, he quickly added, "Or look for something else."

Bessie knew there was nothing else except William's new

house, a stark shell against the bleak prairie. Once the outside walls had been erected, construction had stopped in order for William to help with the harvest. Besides, even though he hadn't come right out and said so, Bessie was sure William had plans of his own for his new house. He spent a great deal of time at one of the neighbor's homes, a neighbor who had a lovely daughter.

That left only. . ."The soddie?" Her voice was a terrified whisper, her thoughts colliding madly with each other until she pressed her hands to her head in an attempt to stop them.

Robert perched beside her on the rock and wrapped an arm around her shoulders. "Bessie, I'm sorry. I thought you were happy here."

She had tried so hard to be a good wife. To keep the house—she refused to use the term to describe the soddie—to keep the place running smoothly in order to help Robert get better quickly. He had interpreted her efforts as contentment!

She jerked to her feet and spun to face him.

"I hate the soddie. I hate the wind. I hate the prairie. I hate everything about this place." Robert's eyes widened and he sat straight and stiff, watching her warily. She knew she must look like a crazy woman, her hands clenched into tight fists, her voice shrill and loud. She was past caring how she looked or sounded, or what he thought. All she wanted was escape.

Her thoughts slowed, her initial panic giving way to blind stubbornness.

"I won't stay here." She lowered her voice. "I won't." Her eyes stung with unshed tears and she welcomed the discomfort. "I don't care what you want."

Slowly, as if all the energy had seeped from his body, Robert got to his feet. Grasping her shoulders, he stared deeply into her eyes. "Bessie, you don't understand. I've never felt like a whole man. It seems like every time I tried to be normal, I got sick. My mother coddled me until I felt like an invalid even when I wasn't sick. Don't you see? I can't go back to that."

She shrugged his hands away from her shoulder and breathing deeply, stared at him without answering. What he said was true, but it didn't change a thing. He had promised to go home when he got better. They didn't have to go back to Toronto or Ottawa. They could start anew someplace else, but when she voiced her thoughts, Robert's face tightened and he stood stiff and straight.

"I've made up my mind." He uttered the words with absolute certainty. "I'm staying. We're both staying."

They faced each other. She could see the gentle pleading behind his firmness, but she ignored it, choosing instead to let her anger well up until it threatened to explode inside her, ripping her to pieces. With a muffled cry, she lifted her skirts and ran toward the soddie. Not until she reached the door and was about to push it open, did she turn to look back at Robert. Shoulders stooped and head bent, he trudged along the path, picking his way back to the hill from which he had recently returned. Slamming the door, she crossed the room in stiff strides and flung herself face down on the bed, letting the scalding tears soak the quilt, her brain burning with anger until she couldn't think. All she could do was weep noisily. Then her anger erupted like a broken dam.

All her waiting was for nothing, all her careful counting of time for nothing, all the patience, all the pleasantness, all the hoping—it was all for nothing. *Nothing. Nothing. Nothing!* The word screamed inside her head like a nail being hammered deeper and deeper. All those times she had told herself that the dark soddie days were just for awhile, it had been a lie.

The pain drove deeper, searing through her body. Crunching the quilt in her fists, she moaned, a sound so deep she wondered that it had come from her. The pain consumed her. She pounded her head into the bed, letting her thoughts continue to rip at her wounded spirit.

She had done everything expected of her. She had cooked and cleaned, and done so cheerfully. She'd made pleasant nourishing meals, canned fruit and vegetables for William, even helped in the big garden he planted. She had done everything, all the time expecting she would get her reward in the end.

It wasn't fair. Why did these things happen to her? There was no reason why she deserved any more or less than the next person, yet life continually threw disasters in her pathway. Why should her husband get sick and have to come to Alberta in the first place?

She thrashed her feet against the bed until she was weary. Her anger burned itself out. Turning onto her back, she stared at the ugly dirt ceiling. The blackness of the sod sifted into her heart

Indeed, why not me? she wondered. She didn't deserve any better. She knew the truth: that although she tried to be a good wife and a good person, inside it was different. She resented the things expected of her, like living in this soddie. There were other things, too. She resented that duty was the only reason for doing much of what she did. Duty. The very word made her lips curl. What did duty have to do with anything? Why not do it out of love? Or respect for each other? Or even call it division of labor? No. It was her duty and she was obliged to do her duty, even though she hated it.

There were days when the only thing that made it bearable was Robert. He never complained or scolded, nor reminded her of her duty. Instead, he would hug her and tell her things would get better. For him she could do her duty out of love and respect. Even though she heard her mother's voice reminding her daily of her duty, her mother wasn't here, so she didn't have to listen. There was only one person she had to listen to right now, and that was Robert.

Poor Robert. She must have upset him terribly with her screaming. She had never before acted like that. She supposed she should thank her mother for that. Early in life, she had drilled it into Bessie's head that a proper lady never screams.

Poor Robert, she thought again. He never spoke of his childhood without a sad note in his voice. She couldn't imagine not having been allowed to race with her brothers or climb trees, or play in the orchard at the back of the house. Secretly, she often wondered if his mother didn't like having him sick and coddled him as a result, but never before had he spoken of it.

She didn't want to be like his mother, using Robert's illness for her advantage. She was glad he felt so much better, and she understood his desire to stay in Alberta, but at the thought of what it meant to her, shivers raced up and down her spine.

Trying to ignore the stain down the center of the quilt, she fixed her eyes on the Dresden Plate pattern. It was almost six months since she'd hung it there. Six months since she'd claimed it as a reminder of home. From the beginning, she had started to measure the time until they could return. How vividly she recalled how she had made the choice to be happy while she waited.

A silent cry filled her heart, echoing inside her head. Was the waiting to continue? Perhaps forever? Could she stand it?

Her place was with her husband. She couldn't bear to be parted from him. She clung to his strength—now physical as well as emotional—with a greediness that was almost frightening. Having made her decision, she sighed and blotched the last of the tears from her eyes.

If Robert was determined to stay then she would make the best of it. There was no point in arguing about it. Hadn't her mother warned her about the folly of arguing with a lawyer? Having been married to Bessie's lawyer father as long as she had, Mother had cause to know.

The black cavity inside her growing steadily, she studied the inside of the soddie, trying to accept that she would be staying. She would find a way to make it work. She could find nothing inside the soddie to give her encouragement. The room was still so small it seemed to breathe in and out when she did. The roof was low and threatening, and it was dark. She couldn't imagine surviving the long dark winter nights. The gloom of the interior settled around her like a weight.

She pushed herself up to sit with her elbows on her knees. How could she face the future? She began to think about living arrangements, hoping to discover within the depths of her subconscious an alternative to living in the soddie.

There was only one other option. William's new house. When had he said it would be ready? This fall? Fall was already upon them and the house needed much done to make it liveable. How many rooms were there to be?

She had paid little attention to the construction other than to admire it when William pointed out something he had done. Not expecting to be there when it was liveable, she hadn't bothered to concern herself. Now she wished she'd listened to discussions about it.

She sat up and looked at the closed door of the soddie as if it held the answers she wanted. Was it possible William would be willing to share his new house with them for the winter? Just until they could find something else, perhaps build themselves a new house? He had said nothing definite about a wedding, so perhaps he was biding his time. She didn't care if the house was finished or not. All that mattered was getting out of the dark soddie.

She would talk to William about it as soon as possible. Or if Robert preferred, she'd let him ask the questions. First, she had to find Robert and tell him what she had decided. She shivered in the damp soddie and thought the gloom had deepened even as she thought about escaping it.

Hurrying to the door, she threw it back, crying out in alarm as it jerked open.

six

A sudden thunder storm had swept across the land. Even now the sun shone through the last scattered raindrops as black clouds rolled away in the west.

Bessie shivered as cold dread tingled up her spine. Robert would be soaked to the skin and cold. Grabbing a shawl to wrap around her shoulders and clutching Robert's coat in her arms, she hurried down the path in search of him. Her shoes were soaked when she spied him wading through the wet grass on the far side of the wheat field, his shoulders hunched, his hair plastered against his head.

Even before she drew close, Bessie knew something had been sapped out of him. She knew it was her fault. If only she hadn't argued with him.

"I'm sorry." She spoke the words as soon as she was close enough for him to hear. "I'll stay here with you. We'll make the best of it. Everything will be fine." She knew she was babbling but something inside raced to explain, to try to undo what had happened. "Forgive me." *Please, don't get sick again. I couldn't stand it.*

"There's nothing to forgive," he said, but his teeth chattered so much his words were garbled.

As she wrapped the coat around him, she gritted her teeth. His skin held the touch of winter's breath.

Thoughts zigzagged through her head, a crazy mixture of fear and anger. She knew this could mean a return of Robert's illness. Anger burned like hot acid inside her head. The fates of life seemed to delight in throwing boulders in her path. But how could she blame fate, or life, or anything else? *It's my own fault. If only I had held my tongue. Mother was right when she said I would live to regret words spoken in anger.*

"Quick," she said, her voice shaking as the smell of wet

wool seeped through his coat. "Let's go home."

Nodding weakly, he let her hurry him toward the soddie where she pushed open the door and guided him inside.

"Take off your wet things while I heat some water. I'll make some tea and fill a hot water bottle. We'll soon have you warmed up. Everything will be right as. . ." She stumbled and couldn't finish. She'd been about to say "as right as rain" when she realized how wrong this rain had been.

Leaving her sentence unfinished, she turned and jammed wood into the stove. The embers were almost dead and she waved her hands above the opening, raising a cloud of ashes. She tried to blow on the red ashes but could only huff ineffec-tively. Forcing herself to be calm, she took two slow breaths then blew a steady stream of air at the embers until a flame licked at the wood. Hurrying so much that she slopped water on her feet, she filled the kettle and set it over the flame. Turning back to Robert, she saw him struggle to undo buttons with fingers that shook so hard he couldn't control them. She hurried to his side, a metallic taste coating her tongue as she reached out to help. Ignoring the way her own hands shook, she unbuttoned his cold wet shirt and pulled it from him. The rest of his clothing followed quickly, though in her haste, her fingers felt stiff and awkward.

All the while, Bessie kept up her racing chatter, promising she would be a good wife, explaining she would be happy to live with William in his new house, or stay in the soddie. She would have promised anything if only Robert didn't get sick again.

Lifting the covers, she helped him crawl into bed and was about to hurry away for the hot water bottle when he captured her hand and pulled her toward him, forcing her to bend over him.

"Bessie," he whispered around his clenched teeth. "I'll be fine. I'm just cold. So cold." His voice faded away to a sigh.

She stared down at him and wished she dared believe him. His grasp on her hand relaxed and she hurried to complete her tasks, filling the hot water bottle and tucking it at his side, warming blankets and wrapping them around him, making tea and lifting his head to help him sip it.

All the time, her insides wound tighter and tighter until she felt brittle.

Even after he fell into a restless, moaning sleep, she paced back and forth—four steps toward the bed, turn, four steps toward the stove, turn, four steps, turn, four steps, turn. She kept it up all night, pausing only to replace the water in the bottle when it cooled, and to explain to William what had happened.

❧

"He's better," she said to William. "His fever has gone and he isn't coughing so much. He's come through fine. It will just take time for him to regain his strength."

William gave her a long steady look then turned and left without speaking. She had seen the pity in his eyes, but chose to ignore it. After nursing Robert day and night for two weeks, through delirium, fever, and wracking cough, she knew he was on the mend. He lay quiet now, the bright spots in his cheeks had faded and he slept peacefully. It didn't matter what William thought.

Quietly, so as not to waken him, she finished cleaning up the supper dishes, all the while promising herself that out of gratitude for Robert's recovery, she would never complain again. She'd learned her lesson. Even if she had to spend the winter in the soddie, she would do it cheerfully. She would do her duty without inner chafing. She would never, ever shout at Robert again.

"Bessie, come here, please." She had been so lost in her thoughts that she jumped at the sound of his voice. Her heart flowing with gratitude at the quiet love she heard in his voice, she hurried to his side.

"Are you finished with your work?" he asked.

She had planned to refill the kettle and set it at the back of the stove in case she needed to make tea for him during the night, but he was so much better that she decided to leave it.

"Then come to bed with me. I want to hold you."

The tension of the past days seeped out her toes, leaving her weak. Despite her firm words to William, and herself, she hadn't really dared to believe Robert was better. Not until now. Suddenly, her heart filled with thanksgiving.

As quickly as she could, she slipped into her night clothes and crawled under the covers and into his arms, nestling herself against his chest, liking the feel of his chin against the top of her head. For a long time, they lay there, just holding each other. She timed her breathing to match his and let herself be soothed by the rise and fall of his chest beneath her cheek.

It was Robert who broke the warm silence. With a sigh, and a tightening of his arms, he whispered into her hair, "Bessie, we need to talk."

She pressed herself into his chest, loathing to end the peace. A skitter of alarm warned her she was about to pay for her deeds and she wished again she could take back all the words and events of that day two weeks ago.

"Bessie, I want you to know how much I love you."

She couldn't breathe. She had expected a gentle scolding, an attempt to explain his decision, but not a confession of love. Tears stung her eyes and she burrowed deeper against him unable to speak around the emotion that welled up.

"No matter what, you must remember that." He shook her gently.

She lifted her head to stare at him, tears making it difficult to focus. "I love you too," she murmured. "So much, so very much."

"I know," he smiled so sweetly that tears flooded down her cheeks. How could he be so gentle after what she'd done?

"I'm so sorry." Her voice cracked. "It's all my fault that you got sick again. I promise I will never again ask to go back to Toronto. I don't care where we live as long as you're well."

"Shh." He pulled her back against his chest, rubbing her shoulder. "It's not your fault."

Choking back sobs, she fought for control. She knew the truth despite his kind words. If they hadn't argued, he wouldn't have gotten this latest cold. She could only be thankful he had gotten over it. A few weeks of rest and he would be fine. *And some good food*, she thought as she felt his thinness beneath her hand.

"All I want is for you to be happy," Robert said.

She jerked her head back to study him. Had he guessed at how unhappy she had been in the soddie? That was before. It didn't matter any more. All that mattered was Robert being well. "I am happy," she assured him. "It doesn't matter where I live as long as I'm with you." He had to understand that the soddie no longer mattered.

He grasped her shoulders and bent his head closer until their noses were almost touching. "I want you to promise me you will be happy even when I'm gone." His gaze was so intense she felt like a fire burned behind his eyes.

Bessie's mouth dropped and then she closed it and swallowed noisily. She didn't know what he meant. His intensity was frightening.

"I. . .you. . ." She took a deep breath and tried again. "Where are you going? You've just gotten over a bad cold and you're too weak to go anywhere." She shook her head. He continued to let his gaze bore into her. Gone! Had he said gone? As in forever? A shot of white hot fear blazed through her. "No!" It was a groan of protest from the pit of her soul. "You're better."

He shook her gently, never taking his eyes from hers. She was powerless to turn away. The truth lay in his eyes, but did she want the truth? She did not. She wanted assurances, promises. Even though she had no faith it them, she longed for words that blessed the future.

"Promise me," he insisted. "Promise me you'll be happy."

She longed for promises from him and here he was demanding them of her.

"Why are you talking like this?" Her words gritted over clenched teeth. "You're frightening me."

He squeezed her shoulders and sighed. "I don't mean to frighten you," he began, "but we don't know what tomorrow might bring." He paused. She knew he hadn't finished and held her breath, dreading what he might say. "I was very sick the last few days, but even when I was delirious, one thought kept bothering me. I was so afraid that if anything happened to me, you would refuse to be comforted, and I couldn't stop worrying about you."

She went limp. He was talking about the past, worried about how he had felt the last few days, and she had been afraid he was discussing the future.

He tipped her head until they were again eyeball to eyeball. "I need you to promise me that wouldn't happen." He was fierce in his intensity. "Promise me you will be happy, no matter what."

She would promise him anything if it made him feel better, so she gave her word.

He seemed satisfied and relaxed against the pillows, pulling her back into his embrace until she was nestled against him from her toes to her head. Wrapping her arms around his waist, she held him close. She couldn't seem to get enough of him, and he seemed equally happy to have her snuggled against him.

They lay thus for a long time, and with each rise and fall of his chest, she grew more and more relaxed, breathing in the scent of him, letting herself become one with him. His breathing grew shallow as he fell asleep and she let her pleasant thoughts lull her as she lay suspended mid-way between calm and sleep. He gasped and drew a long shuddering breath that seemed to come from his toes and last forever. She waited for it to end. It finally did. She waited, but it wasn't repeated. He lay calm and still in her arms. She cradled him closer, willing his body to respond to her love, refusing to accept with her heart what her mind told her.

He was too still. His chest had ceased its life-giving rise and fall.

She clung to him, desperation blinding her to the truth. The pain of acknowledging it was too great and so she ignored it, clutching him in her arms, holding him as if her determination would change the course of events.

She was still in Robert's arms—not asleep, not awake—the

next morning when William pushed the door open, walked toward the bed, and bent over them. Bessie felt his presence more than saw it for she remained clutched to Robert's chest.

"Bessie," William touched her shoulder. "You have to let him go."

At his words, she realized how cold the room had grown. In her arms, Robert felt icy cold. She knew she had to push herself from her dreamy wanderings and see to getting him warm, but her limbs were weak and refused to act.

"Bessie." William's voice was harsh. "You have to get up."

Why can't he leave me alone? I'm so content. It's like I'm drifting on a soft petal, floating across a warm sky.

Only the air was so cold.

Still she could not bring herself back to reality.

William's touch on her shoulder grew more intrusive. He shook her, insisting she get up.

Finally, she groaned and mumbled, "Go away. Leave me alone."

"I can't." With a mutter, he lifted her from the bed.

"What are you doing?" she protested, squirming as she tried to escape his grasp. "I want to stay in bed. I want to be with Robert."

"Bessie." His voice was sharp. "Listen to me. Robert's gone. You can't be with him anymore."

Her struggling stopped and her eyes flew open as she looked into William's face, but there was no sign of teasing, only sober concern.

"I don't know what you're talking about." She turned toward the bed. "He hasn't gone anyplace. He's right there."

William shook his head, and turning her toward the bed, slowly drew her to Robert's side. He lifted her hand and placed it on Robert's cheek. "Bessie, your Robert is gone."

Bessie stood perfectly still, letting the meaning of his words filter through to her brain even as she let the sensation beneath her hand carry its message upward. Robert's cheek was cold and waxy to her touch. Both messages reached her brain at the same instant and her hand jerked back.

"No. . .!" Her wail swelled to a scream.

⋧

"Bessie, get up. There's bath water ready." William's voice hung above her somewhere, distant and hollow.

Bath water? That would explain the thumping and sloshing that had penetrated her dream. She'd been walking along the bank of a river, trees lining the path, dappling the light. . .

"Come on, Bessie." His voice grew closer until his words hung directly over her head. "I'm not going to let you ignore me. It's Christmas, and we're going to spend the day with Tom and Margaret and their family, but not before you have a bath and make yourself decent."

Let him say what he wants. She could ignore him. She turned her thoughts inward to the warm sunny spot where she and Robert had been walking hand in hand.

"Bessie, get up!" The words rang through her head, pulling her back from the spot of light to the darkness around her. Still she kept her eyes closed and refused to answer.

Her bed shook violently and she opened her eyes in surprise, blinking several times to adjust to the yellowish light flickering off the walls. Something stirred in her heart at the sight of the quilt before her, but the feeling died before it had a chance to be named.

"Well at least you opened your eyes. About time." He shook the bed again. "Not good enough though. You have to get up."

"Leave me alone," she moaned, flipping to her stomach and burrowing her face into the pillow.

"Come on, Bessie. Get up!" He grabbed her shoulder and forced her onto her back where she stared into his face.

"Go away!" She wanted to sound angry, but her words held too much whine to convince him.

"Get up." His words were cross but his eyes were gentle. "I mean it. Get up or I'll dump you out on the floor."

She clutched the covers to her chin and glowered at him. "You wouldn't dare."

His eyes narrowed. "I would too, and you know it."

"Oh, very well. I'm getting up." She pushed the cover back

to expose one flannel-clad shoulder.

"You'll have to do better than that."

He was beginning to get on her nerves. His words kept intruding into her cocoon, forcing her to let in a little light, when all she wanted was to hurry back to the warmth and comfort of her shell.

"It's cold," she protested.

"I don't care."

Brother and sister scowled at each other in a battle of wills, a battle for which Bessie had no strength.

"Feet on the floor," the brother insisted.

"No! It's dirty." She turned to him, rounding her eyes, hoping he would soften before her imploring look. Instead, she watched the muscles along his jaw twitch.

"I don't care." He clapped his hands. "Out of bed. Now!"

He barked out the words and she obeyed instantly, dropping her feet to the cold dirt floor. She'd never put her bare feet on the dirt before and loathing rushed up her limbs in a spit of anger. "You're so mean. I hate you." Tears flooded her eyes as she turned to glare at her brother. He grinned at her.

"What's so funny?" She wanted nothing more than to crawl back into bed, or barring that, slap that silly grin off his face. He tweaked her on the nose which did nothing to appease her.

"You," he answered. "It's good to see you still got some fight left."

"Oh. . .oh. . ." she sputtered then gritted her teeth because she could think of no reply, and William's widening grin told her he knew her frustration.

With his hands on her shoulders, he propelled her to the edge of the square tub. Dipping a finger into the water, he announced, "It's still nice and warm." Turning, he plucked his coat off the hook and shrugged into it. "I'll give you thirty minutes and then I'll be back. If you haven't had a bath, I'll. . ." He paused and studied her briefly with an unspoken threat. Turning to go, he paused to glance at her over his shoulder as he stepped outside. "Thirty minutes," he said. "No more. And don't make a mess." He pulled the door shut behind him.

Bessie stared into the water. It was six inches deep in a tub she knew from experience was just big enough for her to sit in crouched like a cat. The cold had crept up her feet to her knees and she hovered between the desire to sit in the warm water as William had commanded or slip between the covers and back into oblivion. She knew her brother well enough to know that he would not give up on rousing her. With a deep sigh, she took off her modest flannel nightie and stepped into the water. For a moment she contemplated slipping beneath the water's surface into oblivion, but the tub was too small to allow such luxuries and within minutes her skin began to pebble with goosebumps. Quickly, she scrubbed herself, dried, and hurried into her warmest dress with stockings and a layer of underwear beneath.

As she dressed, she tried to remember.

She could recall only fragments—blackness that filled her mind; emptiness that tore at her soul; cold that seeped into her being.

William had made the arrangements. She remembered standing at the graveside, allowing people to file by and shake her hand. None of it seemed real. What was real was the cold. It pinched her nose, bit at her legs, and burrowed into her heart.

She remembered Margaret placing a still-warm pie in her hands. She had clung to that patch of warmth.

How she got back to the soddie, she did not know.

William had said something about it being too cold to put her on the train for home. Mother and Dad had sent their condolence and agreed it would be best for her to spend the winter with William. All the time, she had wondered what difference it made.

Consumed with a longing to go bed and get warm, she had wished she could crawl between the covers and block out the world forever.

❧

"Merry Christmas! Come in," Margaret and Tom exclaimed, with the three bright eyed children watching from behind, as they held the door open in welcome. "It's so good to see you."

Bessie closed her eyes, glad to be out of the brittle winter sun bursting off the snow in flashes that stung her eyes and created a burning ache in her forehead, without offering any warmth. Even indoors, the sun ripped through the frost on the window. Bessie turned her back to the searing brightness as Margaret took her coat. "It's been such a long time since. . ." Margaret began.

Since Robert's funeral, Bessie finished silently.

"I've been meaning to visit, but with the cold and snow," Margaret smiled gently, and shrugged.

Bessie silently nodded, and stiffened her spine, remembering Mother's words regarding proper decorum. Never had she appreciated her training as much as now when her senses were assailed with the smell of roast turkey, spicy pumpkin pie, and diapers drying on a line behind the stove; the noise of the children and the snap of burning wood in the stove. It was all so ordinary that it alarmed her. All normal activity should have ceased when Robert died.

A part of her answered Margaret's questions and commented on the lovely decorations and the unique Christmas tree Margaret had fashioned by crocheting coils of green yarn and attaching them to a bare aspen branch. Another part of her, the real Bessie, watched the proceedings, wondering at the enthusiasm of the adults. Didn't they realize that life could not continue the way it had?

"Mommy, is it time now?" little Meggie asked, and Margaret nodded even as she led Bessie to the rocking chair.

The children opened their gifts. Meggie's was a fur muff Margaret had made from the pelt of a pure white rabbit.

"Auntie Bessie, touch it. Isn't it soft?" The child rubbed the fur, soft as an angel's caress, against Bessie's cheek. Inside, unheard by the others in the room, Bessie cried out. There was no remedy for her pain. She could only shut it out and hope to keep it from suffocating her.

Everyone had opened something. There was even a small present from Margaret and Tom for Bessie, a white-covered

Blue Ribbon Cookbook. She thought the festivities were over. They could eat now, and then she could go home and retreat to the warmth of her bed where she knew she would never feel warm again. The cold had seeped through her until it could not be reached by the flames of a fire, or gentled away by the comfort of a thick quilt. She pressed her hand to her forehead. Her head ached from concentrating on the activities and trying to appear interested, even happy. She should have stayed home, and would gladly have done so, if only William had given her that option.

As if he had heard his name in her thoughts, William stood before her. "I have something for you," he said as he shifted from one foot to the other.

"I'm sorry I have nothing for you." One day she had been out walking with Robert. Now it was Christmas Day, and she was unprepared. With a twinge, she thought of the socks she had started knitting for William so long ago. Was it just this past summer? She had lived a whole life time since then. . . and died. But it wasn't she who was dead. She shook her head, confused at the way her thoughts ran in circles, never making sense.

"Bessie." William's voice brought her back to the present. "This isn't from me." He paused and continued softly. "It's from Robert."

"Robert. But Robert's. . ." Was it all a misunderstanding? She half rose from her chair and glanced around.

Seeing her confusion, William raised his hands, begging her to wait. "He bought it a long time ago, when he was feeling well, and gave it to me for safekeeping." He laughed softly. "He was afraid you would find it otherwise." Reaching inside his vest, he pulled out a small square package, wrapped in white tissue paper.

Bessie stared at the gift as he placed it in her hands, her emotions as passive as her body, then lifted her eyes to William, seeking to understand.

"Go ahead, open it." He spoke gently. "It is something Robert wanted you to have."

Robert's scent clung to the paper. She could almost feel him standing next to her. She had been flung backward in time to before the argument, before his last illness, and the speed of her passage left her breathlessly striving for control. Her heart raced, her fingers trembled as she fumbled with the strings. They fell to her lap. Slowly, cautiously, fearing a wrong move would thrust her forward to after that day—to Christmas present—she carefully lifted each flap of paper to reveal a small red velvet case with tiny brass hinges and a tiny brass latch. With fingers that seemed borrowed, she lifted the case and turned it over and over in her hand.

"Open it, Auntie Bessie." Meggie's high pitched voice and Margaret's whispered warning to be quiet startled Bessie. She had forgotten the others were there.

Closing her eyes, she flipped the latch open with her thumbnail. With her heartbeat filling her ears, she looked at the gift.

Against a puff of red satin, on a slender gold chain, lay a heart-shaped pendant decorated with fine filigree.

"It's beautiful," Margaret whispered. "Let's see it on."

Watching a hand that seemed not to be hers, yet moved at her command, Bessie lifted the heart and clasped it in her palm. With a cry, she dropped it back into the box. "It's cold," she wailed. "Cold like me. Everything is so cold." Tears washed her face as she rocked back and forth. "Robert's cold. I know he's cold. I don't want him to be so cold."

Her carefully maintained defenses crumpled as easily as the tissue paper in her fist, and the sorrow she had avoided surged through her with a force that could not be stopped.

Robert—her reason for living—was gone. She had no one to blame but herself. If only she had let Mother's instructions guide her she would never have said those angry words.

The rest of her life yawned cold, dark, and empty.

"There, there," William murmured, patting her on the shoulder.

Poor William. He always seemed to be stuck wiping her tears after she thought her life had fallen apart. Only this time, it really had.

She could see no way to face the future.

Remembering her Mother's admonition about proper decorum, she dredged up the strength to still her tears and smooth her expression. Somehow she made it through the meal, assuring Margaret she was fine now. The activities seemed to go on forever when all she wanted was to return to the forgetfulness of her bed.

seven

William had stoked the fire, lit the lamp and shuffled out with the milk pail while Bessie remained huddled under the covers, watching the fingers of light seep into the black walls. The covers chuffed as she wiggled into a more comfortable position, preparing to bury herself into their warmth for the rest of the day. As she turned, something dug into her breast and she flicked at it with her fingers.

My locket, she thought, catching it in her hand. Suddenly a flood of memories—filled with Robert's sweet presence—swept over her. He had been so kind, so understanding, so strong. She had needed that caring and strength to hold her up. She still did. She was nothing without him. She wrenched at the chain around her neck, her first thought to rip it off and throw it across the room, but wave after wave of loneliness washed through her, and her anger vanished as quickly as a breath in the wind. This was the last gift she would ever have from him. She stiffened as pain stabbed through her. Although seeing the necklace and touching it sharpened the agony of missing him, it held a bittersweetness that made her clutch it in her palm. He had bought it for her before his death, and having received it after he was gone, it seemed like a message from the grave, a sweet reminder of his love.

She moaned—a deep animal sound of despair—and felt a dark blanket of hopelessness draw her to the promise of oblivion. How was she to live without him? It would be easier to lie down and die than to face this vast emptiness of survival.

She rubbed her fingers back and forth over the locket, soothing herself in a mindless infantile stroking rhythm. Something seemed not quite right. The thought registered subconsciously minutes before it developed into a question in her head. There was an unexpected roughness on the back surface. Could it be flawed or damaged? Curious, she unclasped the chain and lifted the locket toward the light. There were markings of some type, but she could not make them out and glowered at the lamplight that puddled weakly on the table and dribbled in splashes to the floor. She wanted to grab the glow and pour it on the locket. She sniffed in annoyance and ending up coughing as she inhaled the smell of William's wool mittens drying behind the stove.

Her desire to know what the scratching was matched her dread of crawling from the warm bed, but she had to know. Slipping into her shoes, she hurried to the stove, wishing the heat would do more than slap her skin. She longed for warmth that would penetrate to her bones, dispelling the cold that had become permanent.

Turning the locket over in her hand until it caught the reluctant light, she saw it was an engraving, and read, *Happiness Always.*

Moaning, she clutched the locket to her throat.

Promise me you'll be happy.

She heard his voice.

Even when I'm gone.

No, she groaned, remembering how blithely she had given her promise. How was she to know it was to be more than just talk? Did he have any idea how difficult it would be? She could barely think about getting out of bed let alone contemplate the idea of being happy. She would never be happy again. She would never be whole again.

She would never forgive herself.

Promise me you'll be happy, no matter what.

I'm sorry, she whispered. *I didn't mean to make a promise I couldn't keep. Please, forgive me.*

There was no reply, no assurance, no forgiveness.

The thick walls isolated her. All she could hear was her own ragged breathing and the echo of her own thoughts. *Guilty.* Just what she deserved.

I'm sorry, Robert, and she swallowed bitter self-loathing. Retrieving the red velvet box in which it had come, she laid the locket carefully back on its satin padding before tucking it into the back of her drawer. She could not wear it. The message on the back was a mockery. The best she could do was pretend.

As the days passed, Bessie discovered it took more than pretense to force herself out of bed every morning; to make herself get dressed, and take over her responsibilities. It took teeth-gritting determination. She alone knew how far she had let herself wander into the black void of mindlessness. She alone knew how difficult it was to face each day filled with self-accusations and lonely emptiness. She knew by the look on William's face that she often missed what he said, and she knew her words often died in the middle of a sentence, but she was powerless to change anything. Survival and pretense were all she could hope for.

She was existing—getting up every day and performing mindless tasks. Happy? She had forgotten what it was.

The changing weather shocked her. She never expected to see spring again. Winter suited her mood, so when the sun grew warmer, the days longer and the first crocuses burst through the melting snow, she was surprised and vaguely annoyed.

One morning after the snow had melted into sloppy puddles, William announced he was going to resume work on his house. Bessie bit her lips to keep from asking him why he would bother. He said he would finish it this summer in time to ask a certain girl to marry him.

"Cecelia Christiansen," he said. "You remember the place where I helped build a house last summer."

He had spent many afternoons even after the house was finished, she remembered. Had he gone over during the winter months? She couldn't remember if he was in the soddie with her or not. The months had passed without memory.

"I've asked a couple of the neighbors to help," he continued. "They'll bunk on the floor in the house while we work, but maybe you could feed them their meals."

Because it took less effort to agree than to do otherwise, she said yes. Besides, the added work would be welcome. It would serve as a prod to help her face each day. Right now there wasn't enough to keep her mind occupied.

William had said they would be there for the noon meal but the first indication of their arrival was the sound of a deep laugh through the half open door. Bessie pressed her hand to her mouth, suddenly afraid. Having two strangers in the soddie would force her to practice her manners—something she hadn't had to think about for months. She wished she'd been able to go back home, but William had explained that the roads were still too soft so she had written a note to Mother and Dad explaining the situation. There had been several letters so she knew what to expect in the reply—stiff words of sympathy accompanied by admonitions to conduct herself properly, remembering her duty, and to be sure to arrange a travelling companion for the return trip. She had given the previous letters the barest glimpse before putting them in a box under the bed—ignoring their words, anxious only to go home. Now she felt a stir of anger. Even in her deep sorrow, she had to remember her duty. For the first time, she was glad she hadn't been able to return home after the funeral. At least they hadn't seen the many days she lay huddled in bed, refusing to listen to William's orders to get up.

She had stared at the pages in her hand, wondering where they expected she should get a travelling companion. She knew of no one who could or would want to accompany her to Toronto. She knew they would expect her to remain with William until "suitable arrangements" could be made. Rather than returning to Toronto and the comforts of home, she was stuck in the soddie about to be invaded by two strangers.

"Come right in." William said, holding the door.

Bessie stared at the first man as he ducked through the doorway. He was a giant of a man. He laughed, and Bessie recognized it as the sound she had heard through the door, a sound so deep it rumbled in her chest, as he looked ruefully at the doorway then slapped William on the shoulder.

"I'd better warn you that one of these days I'll forget to

duck and I'll either rearrange the top of your door or the top of my head." He rubbed his forehead as if to illustrate then brushed aside a black curl that had escaped from the thick waves that showed signs of dampness. She guessed he had brushed his hair just before entering in an unsuccessful attempt to bring it under control.

William smiled up at the man. "I'm not sure which is harder—the door frame or your head, but I expect it would be more work to fix the door."

The big man laughed again. "I'll try to keep that in mind." His smile drew creases all around his eyes and then he turned his attention toward Bessie, as William made the introductions.

"Joe Robertson. A neighbor and a good friend."

Joe held out his big hand. Bessie's first instinct was to back away, but she was already tight against the shelves, so she allowed her hand to disappear into his warm hard grasp.

"I was sorry to hear about your loss." She was forced to look into his face. Eyes so black they appeared to have no pupils bored into hers. She felt herself spiraling downward—or was it upward? She couldn't tell for, inwardly, she had lost her balance. His expression never faltered from that of a kind stranger, but she was sure he had seen right into her soul—seen her pain and guilt, and she longed to get out of the room and find a place to hide, someplace where she could escape this man with the knowing eyes.

"This is Dub Jones."

She jumped at William's words and looked around in surprise, not having heard the second man enter. Joe dropped her hand and turned aside to reveal an awkward youth, who shifted from foot to foot and darted his gaze everywhere but at Bessie.

Throughout the meal, William and Joe kept up a steady conversation. Bessie heard their voices, William's quiet and controlled, Joe's booming and punctuated with chuckles, but their words floated past her. It wasn't that she wasn't interested—or maybe it was, for all they talked about was their work—but his presence made her edgy. He seemed to consume all the space and she felt she had to watch his every move to avoid colliding with him. She wondered if Dub felt the same way for he hovered silently at Joe's side.

As they finished eating and shoved their chairs back, she silently hurried them on their way, anxious to be alone and able to breathe again.

"Mrs. Macleod."

She jumped, alarmed that he had singled her out, hoping to be invisible.

"Mrs. Macleod?"

She lifted her head until their eyes met, and again felt herself spinning. What was there about his eyes that seemed to take away her ability to think?

"Thank you for the nice meal." He smiled and she spun harder, relieved when the door closed behind him leaving her alone to clean up the dishes without his bulk and eyes to disturb the silence to which she had grown accustomed.

As the days passed, she grew increasingly annoyed with Joe. He was too big, too boisterous, too cheerful. He laughed at everything. He loved the wind. He pointed out the pretty clouds. He left crocuses and buffalo beans and harebells in a tin on the wash stand. It was as if he needed to celebrate being alive. Having no reason to celebrate, she found his cheerfulness exasperating.

The way Dub hung on his every word made her cross. Not that Joe was unkind—he gave careful attention to everything Dub said, which wasn't much—and made sure Dub was included in every conversation, even seeking out his opinion.

He ate so much that it alarmed her.

Most annoying of all was his cheerfulness and his attempts to include her in it.

He always thanked her for the meal, mentioning something he especially enjoyed. He had a way of demanding she meet his eyes when she would have rather stared at the wall behind him, or at the table in front.

Then he pushed farther into her world. "Ma'am, you've made this place real nice." He glanced at the newspaper tacked to the wall, now brittle and beginning to curl, and studied the quilt drooping over the bed. "Real nice." He nodded. After a pause, he continued, "I could rehang the quilt for you if you like."

"No," she blurted before she remembered her manners. "Thank you, but it's fine." She and Robert had hung it when they first arrived. It would stay just the way it was.

His eyes narrowed as he watched her. She dipped her head to study her hands as they twisted in her lap, and wished for the hundredth time today alone that he would go away.

When he didn't speak or push back his chair to leave, she raised her head. He was smiling gently, but his eyes filled with such compassion that tears stung the corners of her eyes. "I understand," he spoke quietly, then rose and left the room.

All afternoon, Bessie wondered if she had imagined the expression in his eyes. She didn't want anyone to guess at the depth of her pain. She wanted to hide it even from herself, never to be acknowledged or addressed. She hated him for guessing at her despair.

At supper time, she dreaded more than usual his entry into the soddie, but he ducked in on the heels of laughter. Even Dub laughed, and Bessie turned away, a bitter taste in her mouth.

She didn't want anyone to probe into her sorrow, but their laughter made a mockery of how she felt. As if life could continue, and there could somehow be pleasure left in the world. It was obscene to even consider. A tightness in her chest made her want to choke.

Sleep would not come that night. She longed for Robert with an intensity that left her feeling parched. Nor could she push the emptiness away as she had in the past, burying her head under the covers and pretending it was all a bad dream. Every time she tried, Joe's laughter echoed mockingly through her thoughts arousing heated anger against a man who knew nothing about sorrow. Her anger fueled her misery until it vibrated in the confining room and threatened to consume her.

Finally, tossing the covers back in defeat, and slipping her feet into her shoes, she scuffed across the floor to the light the lamp. Sulfur fumes flared as she struck the match and lifted the chimney. Then a flickering pool of yellow light encircled the table. She hoped no one else would be moving about at this late hour and notice the light through the small window. She did not want to make conversation with anyone—not William and certainly not Joe. She didn't think Dub would venture to the door without an escort for moral support so she didn't have to worry about him. Wrinkling her nose at the pungent smell of the flame, Bessie straightened and rubbed her hands against the fabric of her robe. Pulling out a chair, she lowered herself to its seat, but her bottom barely touched the cold wood before she sprang to her feet again to pace back and forth in the small space between the bed and the stove. Her restless steps did nothing to calm the turbulent emotions within her. Anger raged with grief, equally matched; she felt defeated and a victim of their unrelenting torture. How was she to deal with her life as it loomed before her? The confines of the soddie seemed spacious compared to the way her life had closed in on her. Again, she wished she could have gone back home.

Then she thought of the continual admonitions to do her duty and was grateful she hadn't. It didn't matter where she lived. Whether she went back to Toronto or lived the rest of her life in this narrow, dark soddie, it was all the same in the long run. Nothing mattered anymore.

She wished she had never come to Alberta. All it had offered was false hope and unfulfilled promises, and pain she couldn't face. If only Robert hadn't gotten sick again.

If only I hadn't argued with him. Her own thoughts accused her shrilly, and she stumbled, knowing there was no cure for her guilt. Bitterness raced through her. Life was not supposed to be like this. She hadn't imagined it could be so disappointing, so unrelenting. There was no reason to welcome the future. She dreaded facing another day, and another, and another after that.

Leaning against the shelves, waiting for the weakness in her limbs to go away, Bessie closed her eyes and thought of all the dreams and plans that had died at Robert's death. Marriage, security, a baby. She gasped and blindly filled the dipper with water from the pail, letting the cool metallic-tasting liquid soothe her throat, drowning her thoughts.

She couldn't go on like this—floundering in guilt and pain.

Taking a deep breath, she pushed herself upright and squared her shoulders. She just wouldn't think about it. She would keep busy and not allow herself to feel the pain. She would ignore the inner voice that accused and blamed.

Looking around, she spied the lap desk and decided she might as well use the sleepless hours to write a letter home. Pulling out a sheet of paper, she took the pen from the small drawer and sat at the table. Lost in her thoughts, she twisted the pen round and round in her hand. This was the same pen Robert had used to write his weekly letters to his mother. Bessie had had only one short, blunt note since Robert's death and she knew Mrs. Macleod blamed her even without knowing the details. *Forget it,* she scolded herself. *It doesn't matter what she thinks.* But it did. It hurt that the one woman who had lost as much as she could not bring herself to offer comfort. Robert's mother had never forgiven Bessie for taking Robert from her in the first place, and now the separation was permanent. Bessie could hardly blame Mrs. Macleod for her bitterness. Determined to still her thoughts, Bessie ducked her head and wrote the date on the top of the page.

There would be no entry in Robert's journal for this day.

The thought hit her like a dash of cold water, and she gasped, sitting back in her chair. He had never missed a day, no matter how ill he was. It was as if he captured the day and made it his, and gave it importance by keeping track of it in his writing. Without Robert to catalogue each day, they had blended into nothingness; become meaningless.

Forgetting her intentions to write a letter, Bessie turned toward the packing cases that had served as desk and bookcase for Robert's things. All his books were still in perfect order; his journal laying by itself. She stared at it, caught between feeling an obligation to continue his entries, and a reverence for his belongings that she couldn't quite overcome. Robert had been particularly possessive about his books, especially his journals, and she had never dared touch them except at his invitation when he had shown her a sketch or a sentence. Gingerly, she ran a finger across the front cover of the journal, leaving a bright trail through the layer of dust. She pressed her finger to her lapel, wiping the dust on her robe. A racking chill raced up her spine and she hugged her arms across her chest. It was so cold. Her legs and arms were like ice. Stopping only to blow out the lamp, she hurried to bed, pulling the covers tight around her, and waited for warmth to return—and sleep, to obliterate feeling.

"Bessie. Wake up." Bessie fought her way through a fog of exhaustion as William continued to shake her. Finally, she was able to give a hoarse groan.

"You'll have to hurry," he warned. "The men will be in for breakfast soon."

She stared at him through eyes that refused to focus, her head pounding from lack of sleep. "I'll be right up," she croaked, closing her eyes against the pain searing through her head.

"You look terrible," William told her as he went out. "Better duck your head in cold water before anyone sees you."

"Thanks," she muttered to the closed door, carefully crawling out of bed. A glance in the mirror told her that William was right about her looks and she groaned again. If only she didn't have to cook for Dub and Joe. If only they wouldn't talk to her. Knowing Joe's enjoyment of life and laughter, it was a futile hope. Splashing cold water on her face, she poured a cup of strong coffee to help her face the day.

She grimaced a few minutes later when Joe stomped in, laughing with William. She was too tired to be able to rouse anger, but she felt a twinge of annoyance at his continued exuberance. *Just once,* she thought, *it would be nice if he would come in quiet and subdued.*

"Good morning." He included her in his hearty greeting and she managed a muttered reply.

He studied her with a wide grin and she turned away, annoyed at the twinkle in his eyes. "Well, maybe not for all of us," he amended.

She slopped the porridge into the bowls, not caring that it splatted on the table, and determinedly made no reply. She should have known he would find that equally amusing. When he laughed out loud, she had to ram the spoon back in the pot to keep from throwing it at him. She was in no mood to be teased or cajoled. She wanted nothing more than to be left in peace—or, in this case, misery. She glared at him, silently daring him to pursue the subject and could have sworn he winked before he dropped into his chair and turned to ask William a question.

She sniffed as she took her own place. Although Bessie was quiet throughout the meal, it was not a quiet meal. Dub seemed to have found his tongue for a change and plied Joe with questions about plastering. From the conversation, Bessie understood that Joe was a master plasterer and Dub hoped to learn the trade from him. Although she was content to be ignored, Joe seemed to feel otherwise, for after Dub grew silent and thoughtful, he addressed her, waiting until she lifted her head and met his eyes before he spoke again. Bessie tried to glare at him, but it took too much effort and she settled for keeping a blank expression.

Joe offered his customary thanks though she was sure he was having trouble hiding a smile, then he turned toward the bookshelves. "You have a nice collection of books here, Mrs. Macleod," he said, tipping his head sideways to read the titles.

Did he think an attempt to engage her in conversation would lighten her mood? "They belonged to my husband," she answered coldly, hoping he would consider the topic closed.

"He was a lawyer, wasn't he?" He met her eyes briefly before turning back to his study of the titles.

She grunted but did not answer, feeling her emotions begin to swirl. How dare he talk about Robert like he was simply a lull in the passing of history? How dare Robert leave her alone before they'd had a chance to write their story together.

No, she silently protested. It wasn't Robert's fault. He had done nothing wrong. It was her fault. Joe was pursuing the subject.

"Some of these look pretty interesting." Joe reached out to remove one of the books from the shelf.

She half rose from her chair as she cried, "Stop." The book thudded back into place and Joe's arm dropped to his lap. She could hear the anger and despair in her voice but she didn't care. All she wanted was for him to leave Robert's things alone. She couldn't stand to have someone touch them. "Those are Robert's."

The room had grown deathly still, and Bessie sank back into her chair, not daring to look up. William cleared his throat and pushed back his chair. "I guess we should get to work." He slipped out with Dub treading on his heels. Bessie didn't move. She could feel Joe's presence and knew he was studying her, but she refused to look up. Her heart pounded in her ears as she waited for him to leave.

"Bessie." She jumped, surprised he had used her Christian name. "Bessie, look at me." His voice was so soft that she looked up in spite of the tears stinging her eyes. "I'm sorry." There was no laughter in his eyes, no teasing in his expression, only a gentleness that threatened to unleash the flood of tears Bessie determinedly held back. "I didn't mean to upset you." She stared at him, confused by her emotions. She hated him for upsetting her, for probing into her pain. She wanted to scream at him as if it were his fault. She wanted to scratch and claw at him just to ease the ache, but his expression unsettled her, making her want to rush into his arms and cry against his chest. Shamed by her thoughts, she bit down hard on her lip and turned away.

He pushed his chair back, and jerked to his feet. She jumped as he slapped his leg, but kept her face turned away.

"I'm sorry," he repeated and before she could react, he took two quick steps and strode through the door, leaving her wondering what she should have said or done.

Just leave me alone!

eight

She stared at the dust coating Robert's books. *Burying them in dirt*. With the thought came a mental picture of soil being shoveled over Robert's coffin. Whether a fragment of memory or her imagination, the image propelled her to her feet and she hurried across the room to burrow beneath the bed for the basket of rags. She couldn't let it happen. No more dirt. No more burying. Retrieving a soft bit of tea toweling, she sprinkled water on the cloth, then pulling a chair close to the bookshelves, carefully removed the first, and wiped it clean.

The first section was maroon-covered legal texts that stood like guardian soldiers in matching uniforms. Next to them was a pile of publications. She picked up the first and read, "Government of Alberta Guide to. . ." and turned it over to shake it, coughing as dust clogged her nostrils.

She spent a few minutes arranging the publications in a neat stack then slowly wiped her fingers on the cloth. The only other book on this shelf was Robert's black leather journal, dog-eared at the edges, reminding her of how often he held it in his hands. She could see his long fingers, toiling over the pages, his head bent, his fine blond hair clinging to his head. He would lift his head and smile at her before resuming his task. Squeezing her eyes tight, she held the picture in her mind, treasuring the memory.

She sneezed and scratched her nose. Rearranging the already-dusted books in perfect alignment, she delayed the moment when she must pick up the journal. Robert had never gone far without it, and it seemed offensive that it had lain untouched for five months. Perhaps she should have had it put in his coffin, but she hadn't thought about it until now. She hadn't even allowed her glance to settle on these bookshelves until a few days ago when Joe invaded her life. It had been

Joe's interference that forced her to start this task. Anger swelled against the man who was responsible for her having to deal with Robert's journal. Yet she couldn't continue to neglect it. Robert would have been shocked at its condition. Her breathing grew rapid. She reached out her hand, but then dropped it to her lap. Forcing herself to take a deep breath, she slowly lifted one hand and touched the book, then gritted her teeth and grasped it firmly, slowly lifting it from the shelf. Almost breathless now, she carefully ran her cloth across it, removing the layer of black dust. Her fingers lingered. The cover felt so cold, and lifeless. Suddenly, she moaned and pressed the black journal to her lips.

Robert seemed so close. She could almost see him and hear his voice. It was impossible to believe that he was gone forever. For a moment she rocked back and forth, keening. Her eyes stinging with pain, she dropped the journal to her lap, staring into the distance. As if in a dream, she dipped her head to study the notebook, running her fingers across the cover, wanting the courage to open the pages, to read Robert's word, perhaps finding comfort or encouragement to face a future that was bleak and unwelcoming. Yet she hesitated, dreading the possibility that seeing his life recorded on these pages would serve only to sharpen her pain and increase her despair.

A longing so deep and bottomless that she gasped at its depth filled her with a hunger to touch Robert again—maybe through these pages—and blinking back tears, she opened the book.

His familiar angular writing filled the pages and then the words swam together so she couldn't make them out. She dashed the tears away with the back of her hand and blinked, trying to bring the words into focus. The first page was a list of materials William had purchased for the house, along with the prices he had paid. There were several lines describing the cloud formations that accompanied the weather of the day, and a brief comment about Bessie making stew with meat William had brought home from one of the neighbors. Fresh tears replaced the ones she'd wiped away and with a moan, she slapped the book shut and replaced it on the shelf.

It was no good, she admitted. The journal was only lists and measurements. The words filled her with fresh pain at his loss, but offered nothing to comfort her.

Bitterness stung the back of her throat. She had hoped to find something that would fill the emptiness inside her. Her thoughts darted back and forth, and she jerked to her feet, pacing restlessly in an attempt to keep up with them. Hollowness threatened to consume her. Pressing her hands against her thighs she let them move up and down with the rhythm of her pacing. Jerking her hands away, she folded them across her chest and scrubbed her hands against her elbows then spun on her heel and crossed the floor again, pausing beside the bed to rub her neck. The walls were closing in on her. Suddenly, she couldn't stand to be alone. Throwing open the door, she turned her face toward the sky and closed her eyes, breathing deeply to still the panic that threatened.

Slowly, she drew in her breath, letting the smell of damp earth fill her nostrils. Opening her eyes, she studied the landscape, carefully noting the details. Bright sunshine throwing brittle shadows across the earth, the sky bleached to pale blue, a hint of green along the trail. Caw. Caw. Everything remained the same. Only her life had been turned upside down.

She tipped her head, listening. There it was again. The sound of hammering.

William would be there. She would go over and see the new house. Anything to avoid being alone with her loneliness.

A mushroom smell rose from the damp spots in the path, and she lifted her skirts. Four horses watched her over the corral fence, bits of hay poking out of their mouths. From behind the barn, she heard cows gently lowing.

The new house was pale yellow new lumber. Glass panes replaced the boards that had covered the window openings during the winter and one window was propped open. Through it came the sound of singing. She moved closer, drawn by the deep bass melody, and paused just outside the window, recognizing Joe's voice as he sang, "Someone's in the kitchen with Dinah." Even in song, laughter seemed to bubble close to the surface.

The words died and she heard him speak but could not make out the words, and then he resumed singing in midsentence like he had never been interrupted.

Bessie clasped her hands to her stomach, and closing her eyes, rocked back on her heels, struggling to catch her breath through the pain suffocating her. Spinning on her heels, she raced back to the soddie, feeling more alone and empty than ever, knowing she would never again feel laughter bubbling close to the surface.

Halting at the soddie door, knowing she could not go in and face the mocking reminders of Robert, her only thought was escape, and she turned and fled along the pathway past the wheat field to the hill beyond.

❧

Long shadows crossed the path as she hurried home. Before she skirted the field, she could see three men lined up outside watching her approach, and taking a deep breath, she forced herself to remain calm. As she drew closer, she saw the worry lines in William's forehead.

"I'm sorry," she murmured. "I didn't realize how late it was."

"I was beginning to wonder what had become of you."

Joe stood just behind William, leaning against the door jamb, deceptively calm. Bessie had no choice but to duck past him to enter the soddie. His eyes were intense, and she wiped at her face, wondering if it were streaked from the tears she'd shed up on the hill. She gave him a hard glare, wishing he could be more like Dub, who kept his face turned away from her, edging back as she passed him. Why couldn't Joe respect her privacy?

"Supper will be ready in a minute." Her lips were stiff as she held her head high and hurried inside. Thank goodness, she'd left a pot of stew simmering. It would be thick and ready to serve as soon as she set the table and sliced bread.

William was fast on her heels, following her to the stove.

"Are you well?" His voice was thick with concern, and she felt a pang of guilt at how much he endured because of her. She really should move on, go home, find a position. Maybe she could be a housekeeper, or nanny, and she wrinkled her nose at the thought.

"I'm fine," she assured him. "I went for a walk and lost track of the time. That's all."

"You're sure?"

She nodded and turned to stir the stew. He watched her set the lid on the shelf and bend over to smell the savory aroma. Just before he turned away, he patted her on the shoulder. Straightening slowly, she stared at his back, tears blurring her vision. He had been so good to her. Even before this, she had always known William would take her side in any situation. She didn't deserve his goodness. Somehow, she would make it up to him.

❧

The next day was filled with memories of Robert. Memories that burned, taunted, and accused. She remembered how patient he had been with her fear of the soddie. She recalled his keen interest in the details and uniqueness of the prairie, and how her only response had been disinterest. Now she wished she had cared about his discoveries, had shared his curiosity. Now it was too late. Too late, as well, to withdraw the hasty, angry words she'd spoken. Too late to be sorry. Too late to control her emotions.

She knew she had to learn to control them, but wondered if she ever would as anger raged through like a fire so viciously out of control that it sapped her strength. Why should Robert die? He was such a good man. He didn't deserve to die. A voice reminded her that she had no one to blame but herself. It was her fault for arguing with him. She didn't deny it. She merely wished the voice would be silent so she could find a way to forget what she had done.

The walls closed in on her. The voices inside her head grew unbearably shrill.

Smothering a cry, she ran out the door, not slowing her

steps until she stood before the new house. She hesitated only a heartbeat before she jerked the door open and stepped across the threshold.

The room was silent, filled with the sharp odor of wet plaster. Overhead, she thought she heard a rhythmic scrapping and the low murmur of a voice, and knew by its depth that it was Joe. Dub's higher-pitched voice answered but she could not make out what either said. She guessed they were plastering one of the bedrooms. A tap-tap-tap alerted her to William's whereabouts, also above her head. Relieved that they would not know she was there, Bessie crossed to the far room and looked around. This was her first time inside the house since it was a shell, and she was surprised at how it had changed. This room, with its windows on either side of the door, would be the living room. William would soon be able to bring home a bride—Cecelia. She tried the name again, wondering when she would meet the young lady, knowing William would arrange it at some point. She hoped they would be happy and see the fulfilment of all their dreams. She hoped they would have several healthy, happy babies.

There would be no babies for her and Robert! No fulfilment of dreams, no one with whom to share the future.

Gasping, she staggered to the window, leaning against the wide, unfinished frame, as tears flowed unchecked. Sobs shook her whole body as waves of pain and despair wracked her.

She almost choked when she heard someone clear his throat behind her and she shuddered back a sob. Stiffly facing the window, refusing to turn and face the intruder, she hoped the person would have the decency to go away and leave her to her tears. Sniffing, she let the tears drip from her chin.

"It will get better."

Joe! His words deep and sure.

She could not answer as a fresh spate of tears washed down her face. She did not want to answer. She resented his intrusion and his empty words of assurance. What did he know about how she was feeling?

"I'm not saying the pain will go away, but it won't always be so sharp. Someday your memories will be a comfort."

Forgetting the mess her face was, she turned on him. "What do you know?" She ground the words past clenched teeth. "Have you lost someone so close it's like losing part of your being? Have you wondered why you should live and they die? Have you faced despair so deep it overwhelms you?" She had said more than she intended and clamped her mouth shut. She didn't want him to know how much she hurt, and glowered at him, her fists clenched at her side.

Bleakness so black and deep that it wiped away all trace of his laugh lines filled his face. She jerked back, astonished at what she saw, and uncertain.

"When I was thirteen years old, I saw my father injured in a horrible accident, and for the next two years I watched him die, every day hating myself and the world because I couldn't stop it." He rubbed his hand over his face as if to scrub away memories. "I know what it feels like."

They stared at each other. Bessie wavered between anger at him for pushing his way into her pain, and compassion, knowing the anguish that lay behind his flat tone of voice. Slowly his eyes lost their bleakness and grew gentle, and she felt herself soften.

"I'm sorry," she murmured.

"For a long time I was bitter and angry. I must have been a real heartache to my mother." He paused, his eyes clouding as he thought of his past.

Bessie studied his expression, seeing no sign of the bitterness and anger he spoke of. His face was bright with a hidden joy, stirring a hunger in her heart to know his secret. How had he overcome the pain, and anger? Had he found an elixir that numbed and dulled? If only there was such a potion.

"How did you. . .?" She couldn't ask. It was too personal.

"It was when I realized that God loved me, no matter what, that I could deal with my anger." His face positively glowed.

God? What did God have to do with her pain? She believed

in him, of course, and went to church, or at least she had on special occasions in Toronto, but he always seemed so distant. She shook her head in disbelief and confusion. "I don't understand. What does God care?"

He didn't answer at first, as if seeking for the right words, and then with eyes as black as midnight, he looked deep into her eyes. "One of the hardest things was feeling that I was so alone." She nodded agreement and he went on. "Even though my mother and sister and brother shared the loss, I still felt completely alone inside and overwhelmed by all my feelings. I didn't know how to deal with my pain, let alone my anger at Dad for dying, and my guilt." He stumbled, drew a deep breath, and went on. "When I learned to believe that God loved me, no matter who I was or what I had done, it was like He came inside and shared my pain and helped me sort out my feelings." He shook his head and grinned a wobbly grin. "I'm not saying this well, but somehow his love gave me the strength to deal with it. I can't say it doesn't hurt any more, but it no longer cripples me." His smile widened.

She looked deep into his eyes, drinking in their endless depth, searching them for his meaning. She wanted to believe him. She wanted some cure for her pain, but how could she know what he said was right? How could she be certain God loved her? Certainly, she had heard that God is love, but didn't that mean He loved his creation? He'd created a beautiful world that he was willing to share with men, but they ruined it by sinning, and now mankind as a whole had to be punished. Some individuals deserved more punishment than others. She shuddered, remembering her guilty secret. Yet Joe spoke about love and made God's love sound like such a personal thing. When had she ever seen evidence of it? Not in Robert's illness, and certainly not in his death.

She shook her head in disbelief. "I'm not sure I can believe that."

Joe nodded as if he expected her answer. "It took me a long time to believe it, too." Turning his head to look out the window, his face lit up. "Wait. I want to show you something."

Bounding with enthusiasm, he grabbed her hand and pulled her outside.

Alarmed at his touch, Bessie sputtered in protest, but before she could get her words out, they jerked to a stop outside the door, and he dropped her hand. She relaxed, only to have him grab her shoulders and turn her toward the field. She tried to shrugging him away, but he pointed over her shoulder, oblivious to her discomfort.

"Look at the sky. Where's the sun?"

Trying to ignore the weight of his hand on her shoulder and the warmth where it lay—a sharp contrast to the chill the wind cast on the rest of her, she looked heavenward to a sky filled with grey thick clouds.

"I don't see the sun. It's hidden by the cloud cover."

"Exactly." His voice was triumphant. "Does that mean there is no sun?"

"Of course not. It's just hidden."

"So the sun is shining even when you can't see it?"

"Yes." Even a child knew that. What was he trying to prove?

"It's the same with God's love." He dropped his hand from her shoulder, leaving her exposed to the cold, and stepped around her to stare into her eyes. "He loves us even when we can't see it. Sometimes it's our own feelings that block it out, or maybe events."

As if to prove his point, the clouds parted and the sun blazed through, catching the edges of the clouds in glistening silver, painting the land in vivid contrasts.

She gasped at the beauty of it and a great hunger consumed her heart.

Oh, to find a cure for her pain. She had resented Joe's exuberant enjoyment of life, but how she longed to have just a fraction of that freedom. If only she could solve the problem of her confused emotions.

Joe had been watching her, and nodded knowingly. "Just think about it," he urged. "Remember, the sun is shining even when you can't see it."

Bessie was still staring at the sky when he murmured

good-bye and went back into the house.

Think about it, he'd said, and she did. Even when she didn't want to, it seemed to buzz through her mind. The more she thought about it, the more questions she had. How could a God of love allow bad things to happen? How could he love everyone? How could he love her, especially after what she had done? Could he really comfort her?

By evening, she felt as if she were going to explode from all her questions. She longed to put them to Joe, but hesitated to voice them before William and Dub, and having no wish to be misunderstood, was reluctant to seek Joe out privately, but her questions demanded attention.

Over the supper table, Joe sought her eyes, and asked a silent question of his own. *Have you thought about what I said?* She turned away, keeping her attention on her plate, uncertain how to respond. Would he understand her need? She didn't want attention from him as a man, but she needed to probe his mind on the issues he had raised. She lifted her face and met his eyes. He smiled gently before turning away to speak to Dub. Disappointed, she rose to get the coffee.

The meal was over, and Joe pushed his chair back from the table. Bessie wanted to reach out and press him into his chair, insisting that he deal with the turmoil he had triggered inside her.

"I'm going for a walk before dark," he announced cheerfully. "Seems like too good a day to let it pass unnoticed."

What is so special about this day? Bessie fumed. It was the same as any other. Meals to make, dishes to do. The sun rose and set.

The sun shines even when we don't see it. Just like God's love. Could she believe it?

Her thoughts were in such a tangle that she jerked back in surprise when Joe spoke her name.

"Bessie?" he repeated. "I wonder if you'd like to go for a walk, too?"

She raised startled eyes to him and turned toward William who had picked up a spindle and was sanding it. At Joe's

words, he paused briefly, then resumed his task without looking at either of them.

Her pulse beat in her ears then she scolded herself. There
was nothing unusual in going for a walk on a pleasant evening.

"Just let me get my shawl."

He waited at the door, stepping aside to let her pass.

Outside, he waited until they had walked away from the
shadow of the soddie before he spoke. "I didn't embarrass
you, did I?"

"No. No," she protested.

"Not even a little?" There was a teasing note in his voice,
and she laughed softly as she admitted, "Maybe just a little."
She felt the constraint loosen.

"You looked like you had some questions and I thought this
was the easiest way for us to talk."

The tightness in her chest returned as she wondered how to
voice her questions. By unspoken consent they turned to follow the path connecting the soddie to the barn and other out
buildings. She would have liked to seek the freshness of the
open plain, but under the circumstances, it wouldn't be
appropriate so she contented herself with the alternative.

Joe paused, his eyes seeking the horizon. "There's the
evening star."

Following his gaze, she saw the twinkling star just above
the pink-rimmed horizon.

After an easy silence, he turned to watch her face. "Did you
make a wish?"

She shook her head and he tipped his head toward her, his
eyes catching the last of the light, his gaze so probing she
turned away.

"Why not?"

She twisted her hands as she turned to stare at the barn.
"There's no point in it."

His voice was low. "You won't always feel that way."

Spinning around, she faced him, forgetting all about her
fear of broaching the subject that had plagued her all day.
"How can you be so sure?"

He didn't flinch from her anger, but met her fierce expression with one, that even in the shadows, was filled with certainty. "Because I've been there."

She shook her head, annoyance making her voice tremble. How could he so be convinced? "It's different for everyone."

"Agreed. The details of everyone's loss are unique, but one thing never changes."

She waited for him to continue, hoping he would supply the answers she hungered for.

"God's love. It's always available and always sure."

Bessie sighed. He was so sure. If only it were that easy. "How can you be so certain? Some people are worse than others. How could God love them as much as the decent people?"

Joe remained unaffected by her demanding questions. "Because he came to heal the sick. Those who are well—or think they are—don't need a doctor."

"Some things are unforgivable." She spat the words out.

"Like what?" Still calm in the face of her emotion.

She couldn't tell him. She couldn't expose her own guilt. There were some things that don't deserve forgiveness.

When she didn't answer, his eyes narrowed. "Nothing is unforgivable in God's eyes."

Clenching her hands at her side, she glared at him. "That's hard to accept. I don't know if I can believe it." Blindly, she turned, hurrying along the path toward the corral fence, intent on escaping her tumbling thoughts.

She could never forgive herself, and God certainly wouldn't. She wished she could believe as simply as Joe did. She felt sure it was what gave him the joy she often resented—and longed for. She was destined for a life devoid of either peace or joy. If only she could go back and start again. She would share Robert's interest in the prairie. She would accept her lot and gladly agree to live the rest of her life here. But going back was impossible. Her feet increased their pace.

"Watch the mud." Joe grabbed her elbow and jerked her away from the puddle she'd almost stepped in. Half turned, and off balance, she stumbled against his chest. The smell of

Lifebuoy soap filled her nostrils as his arms on her shoulders steadied her. He was so warm, so solid and strong. Her cheek lay against his chest, the button on his shirt pressing into her cheekbone. Beneath her ear she could hear the steady thump of his heart. She tried to catch her breath but it seemed trapped in her throat and she coughed.

Warmth flooding her cheeks, she pushed herself away, forcing Joe to drop his hands from her shoulder. She faltered, embarrassed and confused and her voice sounded strangely tight as she forced herself to speak. "I'd better get back. I have things to do."

He followed her to the soddie door, never speaking until she grabbed the door handle.

"Good night," he murmured, turning on his heel, to stride across the yard to the new house where his bedroll waited in a corner on the kitchen floor.

With a low moan, Bessie hurried inside.

nine

The soddie was mercifully empty as Bessie leaned against the door, waiting for her racing heartbeat to return to normal. She couldn't believe she had flung herself into his arms so readily. It was, she knew, an action born out of loneliness, despair, and confusion, but that knowledge did little to relieve her hot embarrassment.

Why did Joe bring up the subject of God? she fumed. It was all his fault. If she hadn't being dealing with all those questions, she wouldn't have been so vulnerable or so distracted that the situation had caught her off guard.

Never before had she felt so confused.

She knew it wasn't Joe's fault. He'd simply managed to see past her defenses to the turmoil and longing of her heart—or maybe he just knew it was there from his own experience—and offered what, for him, had been a solution. If only she could find the same peace! This was too easy to be a solution to her problems. She knew, too, she would never scrape up the nerve to tell him why. How could she confess she was responsible for Robert's death? If he knew, his face would close, his eyes grow wary. There would be no more talks of God's love, the sun behind the clouds, or anything. The darkness inside her grew thicker.

Bessie had never told anyone about her guilt. Not even William guessed at the role she'd played in Robert's final illness, and she promised herself he never would. Her loneliness was already frightening in its all-consuming power. She couldn't imagine how much more alone she would feel if anyone discovered her secret. Her friends and family would withdraw. Perhaps not purposely, but they wouldn't be able to help themselves. She would never survive their rejection. The prospect was terrifying.

Having accepted that loneliness was the penalty for her actions, she wondered, yet again, how she would endure it. She needed so badly to be loved.

She pressed her hands to her shoulders where she could still feel the imprint of his hands. The warmth of his chest clung to her cheek. It simply indicated how intense her need, that a man she didn't even like had the power to fill her with such longing. He had done nothing more than offer a few words of comfort.

Filled with disgust for herself, she marched toward the bed, threw off her clothes, put on her nightgown, and burrowed under the covers, where she lay staring open-eyed into the darkness, unable to force her body to relax.

Joe's words about God rushed to the surface. Unable to make sense of the tumbling waves of emotion that accompanied each word she recalled, she flung herself to her side and forced her eyes to pick out the pattern of the shadowed quilt hanging there. She gritted her teeth and counted the barely discernible pieces, seeing them more from memory than from sight in the darkened room.

She awoke the next morning, her head ringing with questions, but wanting nothing more than to slip back into oblivion. She couldn't face Joe. More than that, she couldn't face herself. Questions and accusations roared through her mind.

She made a point of being bent over the stove, stirring the oatmeal, when she heard the men approach and studiously kept her face turned away when they took their places around the table. Nervously, she jumped up several times before she realized Joe was unusually quiet. Unable to restrain her curiosity, she stole a peek at him. He stared at his food, stirring his spoon round and round but eating little.

Bessie swallowed a lump of porridge. Had she offended him? Worse, angered him? Her chest tightened and she lay down her spoon, her appetite gone.

Joe waited until the others had pushed their chairs back and headed out the door before he shoved his own chair back. He hesitated briefly, but long enough for her heart to jerk against her ribs, and then he swung his leg over the chair and strode to the door. Again, he hesitated and her heart turned to stone as she imagined his disgust. He stared out the open door, then turned on his heel and called her name.

She almost dropped the bowl she was removing from the table.

"About last night." He met her eyes with an intensity that made hers water. She teetered on the edge of a black abyss.

"I'm asking you to forgive me. I didn't mean to be improper." He waited.

She swallowed hard, and stared at him, not believing what she had heard. He had done nothing wrong, merely kept her from stepping in the mud. She was the one who had taken advantage of the situation. Wanting to say all this, but unable to get the words past her dry mouth, she continued to stare at him until he shifted uneasily and cleared his throat.

"You did nothing wrong." She managed to get the words out in a jumble. "You have no need to apologize." She was the one who had leaned hungrily against his chest. Her eyes dropped to the button that had pressed into her face and her cheeks warmed.

"Shall we put it down to unfortunate circumstances then?" His words jerked her back to reality and she focused on his face and nodded agreement. A smile began to light his eyes. "Could we continue to be friends?"

She could not tear her gaze away from his black eyes that seemed to probe right into her heart. Into the lonely, dark recesses that cried out for something to fill them.

"I'd like that," she whispered.

His grin wrapped his face in sunshine, and she blinked at the change in him. As he waved and ducked out the door, she hugged the gift of friendship to her heart.

Just before he departed, he assured her that God loved her.

How could he be so certain? She envied him his faith. A hollow cry filled her being as she thought about knowing that sort of unconditional love, but she could never believe that God loved her. *Remember, the sun is shining even when*

we can't see it, Joe had said, but the sun followed a pre-
scribed pathway. It couldn't change its mind, or make judge-
ments. With people it was different, and she was certain it
was different with God. She searched her mind, looking for a
phrase she'd heard, something about the judgement of God
on those who sin. She couldn't remember the exact words,
but she knew it applied to her.

Determinedly, she pushed away the accusations, promising
herself to think of something else, and she did. Immediately,
her traitorous mind returned to scenes of Joe. The way he
turned his head when he talked, the boom of his deep voice,
the rumble of his laughter, the intensity of his eye, the warmth
of his hands.

Grabbing the dishrag, she scrubbed the milk pail as if it
contained slop water rather than a skim of cream from the
morning milking. No matter how busy she kept her hands, her
thoughts raced in endless circles. Joe. God. Love. Round and
round until she felt like screaming for them to be silent.

By the time the men came in for the evening meal, she felt
as if her whole life were spinning madly. Before the men
dropped their bottoms to the chairs, she had filled the mugs
with coffee, than sprung to her feet to offer refills. Twice during the meal, she left the table to remove the towels from the
rack behind the stove and refolded them. Even when William
looked at her quizzically, she couldn't stop herself from repeat-
edly rearranging her knife and fork.

"I think I'll go see how dry the fields are," Joe said, the
sound of his voice making her jump. "Would you care to
accompany me, Bessie?" Her hand skidded across the table,
sending a fork to the floor. She wondered if he was teasing,
but his expression was open and inviting.

Nodding, she retrieved the fork and set it gingerly back on
the table, rose to her feet, stumbling against the chair as she
did. Clearing her throat, she casually said, "I'm sure the air
would do me good." She put down the sudden light-headed
feeling to having risen too quickly.

As they walked toward the wheat field, the sky was pink

with the slanting rays of sunset and the air was gently warm.

"Another warm day," Joe said.

"Yes, it was," she agreed, though in truth, she had paid little attention to the weather. They passed the bluff of trees and Joe flicked a branch through his fingers. "Trees are just about budded out." As they reached the plowed field, he bent over and dug his hands into the soil and she began to think they had come on an agricultural tour. He lifted a fist full to sniff it. "It's time to put the wheat in."

It had been time to put the wheat in when Robert and Bessie arrived last spring. "I can't believe it's a year since. . ." she began, and couldn't go on. She didn't want to remember what one short year had wrought in her life.

Straightening, Joe let the soil sift through his fingers, then dusted his hands on his pant leg. "A year?" When she didn't answer, he asked, "Since you came to Alberta?"

Her throat too tight to speak, she simply nodded.

Joe stepped across the sods at the end of the field. "Why don't we sit here?"

She perched on the cold rocks.

"It hasn't turned out like you expected, has it?" He plucked a straw of dried grass and sucked on it.

Tightness spread up her neck, drawing the skin tight and she couldn't answer his question.

"It's hard to see right now, but God does have a plan—a good plan—for your life."

He watched her out of the corner of his eye as he continued twisting the straw with his tongue.

She shook her head. "I know it's what you believe," she said, watching the straw wave and bob. "I'm glad it gives you comfort, but it's not for me."

The straw stopped its dance. "How can you be so sure?"

She wanted to avoid his question. She wanted to say something simple and dismissive like, I just know it, but his eyes bored into hers and she knew he saw more than she wanted.

A spark of anger flared through the emptiness that was her soul.

"Because it's my fault." Her words were tight, spoken in a low tone.

Watching her with narrowed eyes, he pulled the straw from his mouth and flipped it on the ground beside him. "What do you mean? What's your fault?"

Bessie stared straight ahead, her spine stiff, her hands twisting in her lap, and would not answer.

"You mean Robert's death? You blame yourself for that?" His voice was quiet and low.

Tears sprang to her eyes, but she remained motionless and silent.

"I understood your husband was poorly before you came west." His voice was so low she could barely hear it above the throbbing in her ears. "Wasn't that what brought you here? And the fall weather proved to be too much for his weak lungs."

He waited for her reply. One tear spilt over and trickled down her cheek but she didn't bother to wipe it away, knowing any movement would start a flood. The silence swelled between them. Suddenly, she wanted to explain what had happened. She wanted someone to know what she had done. To hear words of condemnation would be better than hiding her secret any longer. Drawing a shuddering breath, she began. "He seemed better. I thought he was. And I wanted to know when we were going to return to Toronto, but he said we weren't. We were going to stay here."

The pink sky disappeared in a watery fog.

"I'd never thought of staying. It was just until he was better. I hated the prairie, the wind, and, most of all, the soddie. I couldn't stay and I didn't think it was fair of him to say we would."

She turned her tear-streaked face to Joe, pleading with him to. . .to what? Absolve her? Assign penance? Put voice to the accusations that haunted her thoughts?

He didn't flinch. His eyes were kind and gentle and she turned away, confused by his compassion. She knew she didn't deserve it or want it.

"We argued. I said some things I shouldn't have. We were both upset." Her voice cracked and she swallowed several times before she could continue. "I returned to the soddie and he went back up the hill." She nodded to her right to the hill past the wheat field where Robert had spent so much of his time. "Neither of us saw the approaching storm." She shuddered at what came next. "He got thoroughly soaked. He got sick again, and never got better." Her voice died to a whisper.

For several heartbeats, neither spoke. It was Joe who finally broke the silence. "And you blame yourself even though you didn't intend any harm." It was a statement rather than a question.

She spun her head to face him. "I don't expect you to understand. I don't expect anyone to."

His eyes brimmed with an emotion she couldn't identify, and something flickered across his expression. They faced each other tensely and then he sighed and rubbed his hands through his hair. "Oh, I understand. I know all about how it is to feel responsible."

How could he possibly understand her unforgivable guilt? She clamped her jaws tight, and stared at him coldly. He kicked at a sod as the silence stretched between them.

"Remember I said I was thirteen when my father had an accident that lead to his death?"

She nodded but he seemed oblivious of her.

"I loved my Dad. He was so full of life. He made everything an event for us—me, my mother, my older brother, Samuel, and my wee sister, Annie."

He stared at his boot as he continued kicking the clump, but Bessie knew he wasn't seeing the pointless movement of his foot. He was seeing his past.

"Dad worked for Mr. Stewart. Sometimes he took me with him, partly for company, but also because I was already a big lad at thirteen and could help him."

Back and forth his boot swung, sending off wisps of dust.

"I was with him that day. He was hitching Pat and Clyde, the big Percherons, to the stone boat so we could bring in a load of turnips.

"Everything happened so fast, I'm not sure what happened first. The Stewart children had been tormenting the old Tom turkey and had him kinda riled. He flapped past the horses, gobbling and squawking, just as Dad was harnessing them. Pat was younger and more fidgety. As soon as he saw the turkey, he rolled his eyes and screamed. Dad managed to hold them but then the turkey turned and flapped against Pat's legs. He went crazy. Dad called me to help. I was standing right there. I could have reached them and helped hold them down, but I just stood there. I never moved. The horses bolted." He paused, his mouth working. "They ran over him with the stone boat." His voice fell to a groan.

Bessie stared at him, her eyes widening with horror as she imagined the noise and confusion of the scene.

"Both Dad's legs were crushed and he was hurt inside." Joe's voice was low and devoid of expression. "He never worked again. Sometimes I think not being able to work killed him as much as the accident."

Sighing, he gave the clod one final kick, sending it skittering across the ground. "He never blamed me, but I imagined I saw accusation in every look he gave."

"Oh, Joe. I'm sure it wasn't so." But her own silent accusations had been directed at herself for so long, she knew her words meant nothing. She felt a stirring of curiosity. If he was to blame—and surely he did have some guilt to bear—how could he talk of God's love and forgiveness? How had he found the door that allowed him to believe. As if she had voiced the questions aloud, he continued his story.

"I was an angry, bitter young man." His smile was full of regrets. "My parents had taught me about God and love and forgiveness and they sensed what I was feeling and kept reassuring me that God was still a God of love. I don't know how many times they pointed to the clouds and said, 'the sun is shining. . .'"

"Even when you can't see it," she finished for him and was pleased to see his face light up with a smile.

"That's right. But I didn't believe it. I didn't believe it for a long time." Looking upward as if wishing he could forget that period in his life, he sighed then turned toward her, his eyes pleading. She wasn't sure if he was pleading for her to understand his guilt or begging her to believe as he did, but his gaze was intent, compelling her to listen. "In fact, I was on the ship bound for North America before I came to my senses.

"We were in a bad storm and things were pretty rough. I had seen the worried looks on the sailors' faces and began to realize that we were in real danger. I was afraid. I didn't want to die, especially in the ocean, and I knew I wasn't ready. I went to my bunk and stayed there. My mother had given me a Bible, begging me to read it, and that's what I did. Suddenly, it seemed that I was overwhelmed by God's love." Although he looked slightly sheepish at his revelation, he would not break away from Bessie's gaze. She shivered at his intensity.

"It was almost like I could see Him, touch Him. I knew without a doubt that He loved me, and forgave me. All I had to do was forgive myself. All I can say is that it was so real that I've never forgotten it. I promised myself that if we ever got to land safely, I would start a new life. I realized the one thing I could do to make it up to my dad for standing by and not lifting a hand was to never again refuse to help anyone. I've tried my best to live up to that promise."

She shivered, not so much from the coolness of the descending evening as from the force of her emotions, but Joe took it for the former and sprang to his feet. "I'm sorry. I didn't mean to keep you out here until you got cold." He pulled her up. She looked at their clasped hands—hers completely covered by his, so big and warm. She shivered again.

"I'm not cold really," she confessed as they walked toward the soddie. "It's just that your story was so. . .so moving."

"I didn't mean to upset you. I just wanted you to see that I realize what it's like. I admit losing a dad isn't like losing a husband, but I think my feelings of guilt are similar." He looked down at her, his eyes so steady that she blinked. "I don't expect you to suddenly understand about God's love and forgiveness, but I do want you to think about it. Will you do that?"

"I suppose so," she murmured, too confused by everything to think clearly. His story had moved her, made her feel close to him. How could she think about anything else?

And think she did. Late into the night and frantically throughout the next day.

She thought about what Joe said about God and forgiveness. She thought about the pain he had gone through and how he seemed stronger for it. Her thoughts circled round and round. Was it possible to receive forgiveness? There was something hopeful and comforting in both Joe's words and his touch.

Had her mind been more on her surroundings and less on her thoughts the next day, she told herself with some annoyance, she might have paid more attention to the way the men hurried through breakfast and lunch. She had heard the anxious note in William's voice as he talked about it being warm enough to put the seed in the ground. She'd heard Joe's comment that he could finish the plaster if he had a good day, but she'd been too lost in her own thoughts to understand what the men were saying. Work on the house had come to an end, and the men could turn their attention to farm work.

Now, as she stared out the window at Dub and Joe tying bedrolls on their saddles, a gnawing emptiness swelled in her stomach, and she was forced to admit to herself she had grown to count on Joe's presence to break the monotony of her days. It would seem quiet without him. Chances were she would never see him again.

She turned from the window, unable to watch the preparations. Pulling out ingredients, she prepared to make a batch of biscuits.

She measured flour into a bowl and was about to add baking powder when she stared at the bowl in consternation, unable to remember how much flour she had used. Shaking her head in frustration, she dumped the contents of the bowl back in the canister and dipped out a cupful.

A knock on the door interrupted her.

She looked from the cup to the bowl, again having lost count and then turned toward the door, as it slowly opened. Joe stood there, blocking the doorway with his wide shoulders, his hands clasped behind his back.

She couldn't speak, her mouth was as dry as the flour in the cup she held toward him. Hastily, she turned and set it on the table, wiping her hands on her apron before she turned to again face him.

"I wanted to say good-bye before I left," He said, his voice even deeper than usual. "I brought you something."

Bringing his hands from behind his back, he held out a leather-bound book with a soft, worn cover. In a flash, she knew it was his Bible, the one his mother had placed in his hands as he sailed for Canada.

She could feel her heart beating in her ears and, knowing how much this book meant to him, shook her head. "No. I couldn't take it."

His expression grew soft. "I want you to have it. My greatest wish would be that you might find comfort in it."

She pressed her hands against her stomach, still unwilling to accept his gift. He reached out and gently pulled her hand toward him. Turning it palm upward, he pressed the Bible into it.

"Didn't your mother give you this?" Her voice revealed her reluctance.

"She'd understand," he assured her, a wide smile filling his face with sunshine. "She'd want you to have it. I want you to have it."

Still hesitating, caught between reluctance to accept a gift with such emotional value, and a longing to press the book to her cheek, she stared wide-eyed at him.

It was the pressure of his hands that convinced her, and he seemed to know even before her slight nod that she had accepted his gift, and he squeezed her hand in acknowledgement.

"Thank you," she whispered, knowing that words were

inadequate, feeling herself lost in a whirl of sensations as he continued to speak softly, his voice trapping her in a hypnotic lullaby of words as he explained that his job was complete here, and he had to go back to his farm and attend to his own work.

Then he was silent, his eyes so black and intent that she felt herself drowning. Tears stung her eyes, and she blinked them back. Somehow she now clutched the Bible in both her hands. His hands also clasped it, and slowly he raised them. Mesmerized, she watched her hands being raised until they almost touched his mouth, waiting for the moment he would lay his lips against her finger tips. Then he stopped, their hands raised together, clutching the Bible between them. He cleared his throat. "I'd like to visit again if I may?"

She blinked, surprised that he would ask, and filled with trepidation at the implication of his question. Mistaking her silence for reluctance, he lowered his eyes and their hands began to fall.

"That would be fine," she managed to force the words past stiff lips. The sudden light in his eyes made her mouth feel slack.

"I must go. Dub's waiting." For a moment more he stood there. "Read the Psalms first," he said, nodding toward the Bible. "I think you'll find comfort and encouragement in them." Then he dropped his hands from hers and strode across the yard.

ten

Bessie stared after him even when he disappeared out of sight, her hands clutching the Bible, her mind immobilized by a hundred different questions. Why did he give her his Bible? Was it because he wanted her to believe as he did? Why had he asked to visit? Was he trying to help her find the answers to her questions, the solution to dealing with her pain? Was his only concern to convince her to believe as he did? A feeling stirred deep in the pit of her stomach. Was it reluctance or hope? Her grasp tightened on the Bible and a faint, clean smell tickled her nostrils, triggering memories she couldn't identify. The sound of hoofbeats drew her attention, and she looked up in time to see Joe and Dub momentarily appear in her line of vision as they rode out of the yard. Joe twisted in his saddle and looked at her, waving his arm in a wide salute before they disappeared from sight. All that remained was a grey cloud kicked up by the horses.

It was at that moment she identified the memory stirred by the aroma from the Bible. The evening she had clung to him, she had noticed the pleasant smell of the soap he used. The same aroma rose from the covers of his Bible, probably from its being carried close to him.

Will I ever see him again? Knowing she might not, she turned back to face the dark, silent room, a wave of despair making her shudder.

Already she felt Joe's absence. He was so big that his leaving left a vast empty feeling even in this tiny room where he always seemed to hunker down to keep from pushing out the walls. Turning her face upward, she studied the door frame that had been a continual threat. Somehow he had avoided cracking his head on it.

He asked if he could call. Could it be—she pressed the Bible to her again—could it be that he cared? Did she want him to? Robert had cared, but that was such a long time ago. She had convinced herself no one could ever care again because of what she had done. A trickle of hope seeped into her heart even as she scolded herself for being foolish. Sighing because hope and despair seemed hopelessly tangled, she told herself it was time to turn back to preparing the evening meal for William.

First, she had to find a safe place to put this special gift from Joe. She studied the book in her hands. The cover was worn to a soft suede, and she resisted an urge to rub her cheek against it. As she rubbed her fingers along the surface, she detected a slight depression. At first she was puzzled about it, then pictured Joe's hand grasping the book and knew it was the impression of his thumb.

For several heartbeats, she stroked the soft leather, thinking about how much this book meant to Joe. A part of her—the curious part—wanted to open the pages and see what secrets she could discover; another part shied away at snooping.

He gave it to me to read, she reminded herself, and slowly turned back the top cover. The pages were tattered, the edges darkened from use. It was a book that had been much read, its pages often turned. She flipped a few leaves and saw that he had made notes in the margin. Bold black letters that read, *Amen!, That's me,* or a date. Her breath came in quick jerks and she felt herself growing warm as if caught reading someone's personal mail. In fact, that's exactly how she felt. A snoop. An eavesdropper. She could almost feel Joe's eyes boring into hers, accusingly.

Wait. What had he said? "I want you to have it." Those were his exact words. She knew she hadn't imagined it. Her embarrassment gave way to anticipation. Maybe it was possible to find Joe's peace and joy in life. Maybe the answers were here. He seemed to think so. She hurried to the dresser and carefully laid the Bible on the runner. Just as soon as she had a moment she would begin searching the pages for answers, both to her own troubling problems, and, she admitted quietly to herself, to who Joe was and what made him so confident.

ঌ

It was mid-morning the next day before Bessie got her chance to open the pages in Joe's Bible.

"I'm off to town to see to a bit of business," William had announced a few minutes ago. "I won't be back until late. Don't bother with supper for me. I'll probably eat at Christiansens'."

Bessie smiled to herself at the anticipation on William's face. "So when do I get to meet Miss Cecelia?" she teased, her smile widening as William stared into the distance, having forgotten her. "William?" Her voice jerked him back to reality.

"Hmm? Oh yes." He cleared his throat to cover his discomfort. "I'll bring her over as soon as the seed is in. Maybe we could have a picnic or something."

"Just let me know." She waved as he rode out of the yard.

The whole day to herself. A perfect opportunity to steal a few minutes to have a look in Joe's Bible. She took it from the dresser and looked around the soddie. It was too close and confining; the light too poor for good reading, and she hurried outside intending to find a place along the side of the soddie where Robert had so often sat, but it didn't feel right. It wasn't that she didn't want to be close to Robert's memory, but it made her restless to think of sitting in his favorite spot. Crossing the yard, she perched on a rock at the edge of the plowed field, but again, restlessness made her bound to her feet and walk toward the hill. Without planning it, she followed the pathway up the hill until she stood on the crest looking down on the bright clear colors of spring. The hint of green peeked through last years' grass and a flash of blue reflected the sun. For several minutes, she studied the scene, as waves of memories washed over her. This was where Robert had spent many afternoons, filling his senses with the vastness of the prairie that had made him feel more of a man than he had previously. She closed her eyes in regret and moaned quietly. Why hadn't she been able to understand that a year ago? Why had she been so slow to see? She would have given anything to go back and undo the selfish things of last summer.

It was too late. Robert was gone forever. At least he would never have to suffer another bout of choking lung fever. With that she consoled herself as best she could. She had accepted that her life must go on without Robert, and tainted by her guilt. Somehow she would have to find a way of using that bitter lesson for good, though at the moment she could think of no positive thing that could come from it other than a severe warning to hold her tongue. Her own selfishness in instigating the argument between them would always haunt her. *I've learned my lesson,* she vowed, knowing there was less certainty than prayer in her words.

Turning her attention to the Bible in her hands, she wondered again if it held the power that Joe would have her believe.

Finding a dry grassy place, she sat down, shifting about until her legs were drawn up comfortably and her skirts arranged, then she opened the pages, cool and smooth as satin, and felt herself drawn to the book in a way she couldn't understand. Perhaps it was reverence because she had been taught the Bible was holy. Perhaps it was desperation, for she realized today, for the first time since Robert's death, that she was ready to move forward with her life, yet was unsure how. Whatever the reason, she was eager to discover the secrets of Joe's Bible.

He had said to begin in the Psalms. She had heard of them, of course, but flipped a few pages before she located the first chapter and began to read, "Blessed is the man. . ." Or woman, she added, as a great yearning swelled inside her heart. This indeed was what she longed for—blessing instead of accusation. She continued reading, the word pictures drawing her up and away from life which she had found to be so full of pain, to a world of majesty and power and beauty. Tears rolled unheeded down her cheeks as she read the words, "I laid me down and slept; I awaken; for the Lord sustained me." How often had she lain awake, staring up at the dark earthen ceiling, seeing nothing, yet tormented by scenes that would not let her rest? The promise of sleep and being sustained were worth more to her than all the gold in the world, and when a bit further on, she read similar words, "Thou hast put gladness in my heart, more than in the time that their corn and their wine increased. I will both lay me down in peace, and sleep; for thou, Lord, only makest me dwell in safety," she pressed her fingers to her mouth, and smothered a cry.

Peace. Safety. Sleep. Gladness. The words rang inside her head like bells on Sunday morning. No! More. Like the bells at the birth of a child—joyous celebration.

Dashing the tears from her eyes, she looked out across the land. She saw the vibrant colors of new life, and breathing deeply, drank in the fresh April scent of new growth. Spring had come. A time of beginnings.

Was it possible for her to have a new beginning? Perhaps that was wishing for too much. She would be satisfied with peace, safety, sleep. And just a touch of gladness.

Bending her head, she resumed reading, each word touching a chord in her heart, sometimes of joy, sometimes of hope, sometimes of sorrow.

At chapter eighteen, she read, "The Lord is my rock. . .my fortress. . .my deliverer. . .my salvation. . .my high tower," and her focus shifted from an inward look to a consideration of God. Was it possible that He could be all those things to her. Or was this for the writer? Did she dare hope?

With a deep sigh she closed the pages and rose from the ground surprised at how stiff she felt. Looking about her, she saw the sun had moved toward the west, laying long shadows across the land. She had been there longer than she thought possible and hurried down the hill thankful she didn't have to make supper for William.

A few days later, she made a trip to town, anticipating a visit with Margaret, yet feeling a strange reluctance to give up the time she could have otherwise used for reading.

Margaret was her usual self, bubbling with tidbits of news and nonsense even as she dashed after Benny who now ran helter skelter from one piece of mischief to the next. Bessie wondered if Margaret was made of elastic the way she bounced up and down to waylay Benny before he pulled some object down on his head, or climbed on a chair teetering dangerously.

As Margaret made tea, she set out a basin of potatoes to peel.

"I'll help," Bessie offered, picking up a knife and taking over the task as the young mother dashed after Benny again.

"How is the new house coming?" Margaret asked as soon as she caught her breath. It had been weeks since their last visit and Bessie described the progress.

"It looks to me to be almost ready to move into," she finished.

Margaret looked at her with narrowed eyes. "Has William any special plans?"

Bessie nodded. "He spends a lot of time at the Christiansen place and talks a lot about Cecelia. I expect he's hoping to share the new house with a new bride."

"And what are your plans?"

She and William had discussed it just the other day and he had asked her to put off making arrangements to travel until he contacted Mother and Father. She knew he hoped their parents would come west for his wedding.

"It would be best if you waited and travelled with them," he pointed out.

Bessie told Margaret all this.

"You had Joe Robertson out there helping." Margaret watched her curiously, as Bessie studiously continued peeling potatoes. "What a big handsome man. Tell me, what is he like?"

Bessie laughed. "He's. . .big."

Margaret laughed, too. "He is, isn't he? I'm afraid I sometimes stare at him rudely, but what else?"

"Well. . ." She measured her response, not wanting to be misunderstood. "He laughs a lot. And he teases, but he seems to care about people."

Margaret nodded as if the answer satisfied her. "I hear he's a real good neighbor. He did the chores for the Macleans when they were all sick last winter. They had a bad bout of flu and weren't able to manage for a week or more. It's quite a thing for a man to take on two sets of chores, especially considering the weather. It was frightfully cold right about then. And he took his wagon and went all the way to Berchewan to help Mr. Kuyper bring home the lumber for their house. Seems he's willing to do most anything to help a body out."

Bessie nodded, knowing that was exactly how Joe felt, but she couldn't think of Joe without thinking of his Bible, and curious as to what Margaret thought, she asked, "Have you ever read the Bible?"

She hadn't expected tears, and began to apologize but Margaret lifted her hand. "I'm fine. It's just that you touched a tender spot. I have read the Bible. I was raised to do so and to obey it, but somehow along the way I've let things slide. I guess it was when we came west and there was no church and no parents to remind us of what we should do. The truth is we got busy with other things. We seem to have forgotten what was important. Just the other day, Tom and I were saying it didn't seem right—the way we'd neglected God. I've been feeling sort of. . .well, I suppose it's restless for quite awhile." She paused and took a deep breath, wiping the tears off her cheeks. For a moment they were both quiet, lost in their thoughts then Margaret turned to Bessie. "What made you ask?"

Haltingly at first, Bessie related how Joe had left his Bible for her to read, saying it would reveal God's love.

❧

Margaret had nodded in agreement, Bessie recalled as she followed the pathway home, and had spent the rest of the afternoon telling her about the times God's protection and help had been evident, even when they hadn't thought of Him for days.

"He makes my life secure," Margaret had explained, her eyes revealing the depth of her feelings.

Mindless of the road her feet trod, Bessie considered

Margaret's words, wondering what it would be like to know the kind of security that made ones eyes glisten. She thought about the warring emotions that had twisted and boiled all winter—a tangled mess of guilt, anger, resentment, and despair. She stumbled and stopped walking, pressing her palm to her heart. Their sting was gone. When and how it had happened she couldn't say, but quietly and certainly, her turmoil had been soothed as if an invisible hand had smoothed it away.

"It was God," she said aloud. "He does love me." She wrapped her arms around herself, laughing like she never had before, a bubbling joy from deep inside.

Her joy grew silent and she looked around, seeing the prairie landscape as if for the first time. The sky was so clear and blue, she felt she had glimpsed God's dwelling and smiled at the thought of His majesty. Dropping her gaze, she watched the new leaves on branches that swayed and bent in the breeze and thought of the verses that said the fruit trees and the cedars praised the Lord. "Why the trees are worshipping you," she spoke aloud, addressing her words to God.

The tips of the branches touched and parted, back and forth, like clapping.

"O clap your hands, all ye people." The words sprang sharp and clear into her mind, and she was overwhelmed with the beauty of nature rejoicing before God. Falling on her knees, she raised her hands heavenward lifting her heart toward God in harmony with creation.

Joy flooded her being and she laughed and cried then grew quiet, feeling something in her soul germinate and grow, vibrating with life.

❧

The joy and peace of that afternoon remained with her throughout the following days and must have been evident on her face for one morning William looked at her closely, following her every move with his eyes. Finally, his brow wrinkled, he asked, "What's come over you? You seem different."

Dropping to the chair opposite him, she tipped her head

and smiled. "In what way?" she teased.

His eyes narrowed, and he leaned across the table, peering into her eyes. "You seem happier." He shook his head and sat back. "I just can't put my finger on it."

"Want me to tell you?"

He nodded, his expression cautious.

"Well," she began hesitantly, not sure where to begin. "When Joe was here, he told me God loved me and cared how much I was hurting. When he left, he gave me his Bible and asked me to read it." She paused, willing her brother to understand and be happy for her. "I have been—reading it. And I've found that Joe was right. God does care."

William sighed and relaxed. "Is that all? Sounds harmless enough to me." He pushed to his feet and grabbed his hat as he left.

Disappointed by his lack of enthusiasm, she stared after him. What had she expected? Shrugging, she rose from the table and scooped up the Bible from its customary spot on top of her dresser, heading out doors. It had become her habit to hike to the top of the hill to read. Today was no different except for one thing. Yesterday she had finished the Psalms and at the end discovered a note from Joe.

> *Bessie, if you read this it will be because you have read the Bible as I hoped and prayed you would. I hope you have found peace and comfort in reading the Psalms. Try reading the Gospel of John next. I think you'll find it contains a message just for you.*
>
> *Joe*

Bessie had run her fingers over the bold, black words, feeling Joe very close. She could see his hands, so long and strong, holding the pen that wrote this message. The scent of the soap he used touched her nostrils, and she told herself it was because it clung to the page upon which he had written, but she knew it was in her memory.

Loneliness sucked at her innards. She longed to see Joe, and talk to him; share her discoveries and thank him for leaving his Bible.

That was yesterday.

She was bursting to explore further in Joe's Bible.

Using the index, it took a few minutes to find John's Gospel. Staring up at her from the first page was another message from Joe. At first the words swam and she blinked hard to bring them into focus.

> *Bessie,*
> *God loves you as I hope you have discovered*
> *already, but He has so much more in store.*

He listed several verses from John and she eagerly looked them up, lingering over their message, then returned to Joe's note.

> *See, there is forgiveness. God does not condemn;*
> *He forgives. You have only to believe it to receive it.*
> *My prayer is that you will discover these truths for*
> *yourself as you read John.*

> *Joe*

She read the message again, lingering over each word, hearing Joe's deep voice speak, and then she began to read John. It was not a long book and she read it straight through before she looked up.

Staring out across the vast landscape, she thought of all the times she had read "Whoever believes" and the promises made to that person: living water, eternal life.

Turning back to Joe's message, she read it again.

> *You have only to believe to receive it.*

It was no longer hard to believe. She was now certain God would forgive her for her part in Robert's death, though she would find it harder to forgive herself. She wanted the life and joy and peace that were promised as a part of believing.

Knowing that what she was preparing to do was momentous, she laid the Bible carefully on the ground and knelt beside it.

"I believe and I receive." She could say no more as her heart overflowed with emotion. For a long time she knelt there, pouring out her heart to God and feeling His healing flow deep into her being.

As she rose to make her way down the hillside, she paused to stare across the valley. Somewhere over there, Joe lived.

"Joe," she whispered. "You said you'd come."

eleven

The sun beat down on Bessie's head, making her hot and sweaty. *If only these weeds weren't so stubborn,* and she slashed at them with her hoe.

A year ago she would have been chaffing at the hardship of pioneer life, but today her biggest concern was the tender blisters forming on the palms of her hands.

Wiping her brow with the back of her hand, she pushed a strand of hair off her face then attacked another clump of stubborn grass that threatened to choke out a tender bean plant.

She wouldn't be here to see the potatoes dug, nor the grain harvested, she thought.

Three weeks ago William had finally brought Cecelia over to visit. Bessie had immediately liked this fair-haired quiet girl who followed William's every move with her eyes and dimpled at him when he spoke. Bessie soon discovered Cecelia had a quiet sense of humor that elicited low chuckles from William. It was good to see them together, Bessie thought and wished them nothing but the best. After tea and cake, William and Cecelia had gone to the new house. Sometime later they returned, hand in hand, Cecelia dreamy eyed and William striding confidently.

"Bessie." He drew Cecelia closer to his side. "We have decided to get married mid-August."

William had immediately written their parents, and plans were made for them to come west for the wedding. Afterwards, Bessie would accompany them back to Toronto. It was less than three months away. She could find no enthusiasm for going back home. She'd grown used to the living conditions, the prairies, and almost even the soddie.

Since her encounter with the God who loved her, a sense of peace pervaded her life. It was as if she were quietly waiting—

for what she hadn't attempted to guess—not unsettled by her lack of knowledge. For now, it was enough to enjoy her new-found peace.

If only she could see Joe before she left. It was almost six weeks since he rode out of the yard—and apparently, out of her life. In that time she had neither seen him, nor heard from him, and she accepted that she probably never would. She could write him a note thanking him for his Bible and telling him that she now believed, but was reluctant to do so. What she wanted was to look into his face as she told him and see his dark eyes gleam with pleasure.

Straightening, she looked down the row she had completed, and sighed. She had promised herself she would complete this task today even if it took all afternoon, and it looked like it would. Stepping across the next row of plants, she began again.

Her blisters were growing more painful and she paused to study them. Gritting her teeth, she tried to hook her thumb around the hoe handle and thus avoid the tender areas, but as she hacked at the defiant grass, the hoe flipped out of her hands.

"I will finish this," she muttered as she bent to pick it up. "I don't care how long it takes." She went back to the task.

"It's a hot day for such hard work."

Bessie dropped the hoe and yelped as she spun to face the speaker. Joe sat astride his big bay horse, leaning casually forward on the horse's neck.

"Hello, Bessie."

She had forgotten how big he was. He filled her vision except for a narrow frame of pale blue sky that accentuated his darkness. The summer sun had bronzed his skin. His eyes were shaded by his worn cowboy hat.

She closed her mouth and swallowed, but her voice seemed to have vanished. The horse stomped his feet and blew a warm spray from his nostrils. Nearby a meadowlark fluted its clear song.

Joe removed his hat freeing a lock of wavy black hair to

droop across his forehead. His hair had grown since she last saw him and it curled around his ears. She could now see his eyes, black and intense, studying her unblinkingly.

"Bessie?" he said, uncertainly.

She took a deep, steadying breath. "Where did you come from?"

Throwing his leg across the saddle, he slid to the ground, and the sky returned, bright enough to make her to blink.

"From home."

"Of course." Confused by his sudden appearance, her mind had turned to cotton.

Joe bent to retrieve the hoe. "I'll give you a hand."

Setting a pace that left her staring at his back, Joe cut the weeds down with precision. His sleeves, rolled up to his biceps, revealed cords of muscle that bulged and rippled. She blinked. Within minutes, he had finished what would have taken her most of the afternoon, and he turned and walked back the newly cultivated path.

He reached her side and gathered up the reins. "Let's go sit in the shade and talk." He waited for her to fall in step with him.

❧

Bessie forced herself to watch the fluttering flight of a brown butterfly, and when it disappeared from sight, she pointedly considered the lazy white clouds that hung unmoving in the afternoon heat. Despite her determination not to let it happen again, her eyes drifted down to where Joe, having refused her offer of a chair, lay stretched out on the ground before her, one leg bent, the other straight.

Shifting over onto one elbow, he looked at her. "I planned to come sooner, but things got busy." She nodded silently. "It took me longer than I planned to plant my own crop because I broke the hitch from the dicer and had to get it repaired." He plucked a blade of grass and ran it through his fingers. "Then I went over to help the Kuypers with their crop. Lo and behold, if their old plow horse didn't pick right in the middle of the first field to up and die. Course she's been on her last legs for ages, but seeing it was their only horse, I didn't have much choice but to take Fred—Mr. Kuyper—looking for a new horse." He chuckled. "And didn't he go and buy one just as decrepit."

His low laugh did strange things to Bessie, things she couldn't believe. A burst of longing broke inside her heart as she thought how she'd like to listen to that sound every day of her life, and she began to see him with new eyes.

She'd never noticed before the way his eyes seemed to change with his words and emotions. Black as ink, they were one minute bright and shiny like a piece of hardest coal; the next, soft as the fur on the old black barn cat. Once she caught a shadowed look that stabbed at her heart.

His face was so mobile. It was browner now than when he had been there to help with William's house, with lines spraying outward from his eyes like a burst of laughter. His wide smiling mouth drove dimples deep into each cheek.

It was as if she was seeing him for the first time, and she felt awkward at the confusion of emotions she felt.

Joe's voice broke into her reverie. "Has William done more work on the house?"

Glad of a reason to escape her thoughts, she filled him in on what had transpired. "It's all but finished," she concluded. "He and Cecelia ordered a new stove last week. Her parents have volunteered some basic furniture, and William plans to make some things."

"Have they set a date then?"

"August fifteenth." Her deadline too. After that she'd be gone. The thought seemed suddenly depressing.

Joe studied her face, his eyes turning soft as fur. "Bessie," he began, his voice gentle. "I've thought of you so often and wondered how things were with you."

"I'm fine. Much better." She had been so full of what she wanted to tell him, but it had all fled, leaving her rattled and virtually tongue-tied.

Joe dropped his gaze for a minute. When he looked up, his eyes were bright and direct. "Did you read my Bible?"

She nodded, finding herself wanting to look away from his piercing gaze, but trapped by his intensity. "I did. I've been wanting a chance to thank you for lending it to me."

He waved aside her thanks, his eyes never wavering from hers. "I've prayed you would find what you needed as you read it. Did you?"

She took a deep breath. "I did. I found so much more than I expected." Hesitantly at first, and then with growing confidence as his eyes never wavered, she told him how the majesty and power of the words had lighted the dark corners of her heart and filled her with hope. She related how she had read his message about forgiveness, and after reading John, had made a decision to believe it.

By the time she finished her story, Joe was sitting upright, his arms wrapped around his drawn up knees, leaning toward her, his eyes never leaving her face, as if it was vitally important not only to catch every word, but every nuance of her expression as well.

"Everything you said is true," she concluded. "God's love is so real. It's given me comfort, forgiveness, and peace beyond imagination."

Relaxing suddenly, Joe leaned back on his elbows. "I'm glad for you." His smile widened, filling his eyes with flashes of light. "I know it's been the greatest discovery of my life."

His dimples drove deep into each cheek and she answered with a smile she couldn't contain. Between them something strong and tender was born; the sure bond that comes from having common feelings on a deeply intimate subject.

"Bessie." His voice deepened with emotion as he leaned toward her.

She felt herself drawn to him, bending forward slowly.

Hoofbeats thudded across the yard.

William! Bessie jumped up in guilty confusion. Where had the afternoon gone? She'd done nothing about preparing William's meal.

She had forgotten her duty.

She smiled and almost chuckled aloud, because she discovered she didn't care.

"How do, Joe," William called.

"William." Joe rose to his feet and brushed his clothes off before he held out his hand to his neighbor.

"Staying for supper?" William invited.

Bessie held her breath, and then wilted as Joe answered, "Can't. I'm doing chores at the Kuypers for a few days and I'll have to hurry if I'm to get them done before nightfall." He picked up his hat and banged the grass off on his thigh. "I'll be back though." He waited until Bessie met his eyes before he slapped his hat on and crossed the yard to where he had tied his horse.

&

He wasn't coming, despite his final words. He had no reason to return.

She had told herself so a hundred times over the past three days, trying unsuccessfully to convince herself. She shouldn't be surprised or disappointed.

Yet she kept returning to the window to check for a trail of dust along the road, and when she was outside, she paused often, wondering if she heard the thud of horse hooves.

Even now as she pulled the door shut behind her, she bent her ear, listening, and glanced down the road, waiting for some sign. Sighing, she picked up her basket and set off down the road toward town.

Why should it matter if he called again or not? He was just showing kindness to a sorrowing widow. She mocked herself with her words.

But it did matter, and she was at a loss to explain why.

Her emotions were such a complicated mess. Gratitude for Joe's concern, for his having shared his Bible, and for his part in showing her God's love. Such knowledge still thrilled and awed her, but there was still more in her heart when she thought of Joe. He was a man who lent himself to others. She knew how much time and effort he spent helping his neighbors. He had once told her how he'd promised himself he would never pass up an opportunity to help someone if he could. She knew he did it in memory of his dad, but it seemed as if he thrived on lending a hand whenever he could and she admired him for that.

She longed for his friendship. He seemed to be able to look into her eyes and read her heart and, while seeing the ugly as well as the good, still care. He had a knack of making her feel secure and she hungered for more of his frank acceptance. She knew she couldn't expect Joe to understand her needs. It wasn't his responsibility. Nor, she was quite certain, was it his concern.

There was only one thing that mattered and it had been accomplished. She had expressed her thanks as best she could and he had accepted it. She had nothing more to wish for. So why did she feel this strange restlessness when the days passed and he didn't call? Why did her eyes seek the road even when she was determined not to look again? She provided her own answer. She was acting like a foolish school girl. It was time to grow up. She would go to town, look after her business, return home, and forget all about Joe.

❧

She swung her basket and hummed as she marched along. *Perhaps he's had to go over and help the Kuypers again. It seems to take quite a bit of his time.* She stomped her foot and forced her thoughts to wedding plans. Already the new stove was in the house and several pieces of furniture. Cecelia came over often, measuring windows, and dreamily pacing the floor, saying how nice the house was. William and Cecelia had asked her to stand up as one of their witnesses, and she was having a new dress made at Millie's for the occasion. She was happy for them, yet almost dreading the date.

I should be looking forward to returning home, she mused, but she wasn't. For one thing, she would be returning as a widow—Robert gone forever. Pain shot through her heart making her gasp. Would she ever be able to think of Robert without a stab of pain and a fresh surge of guilt? Perhaps not. All she could do was remind herself that God loved her no matter what she had done.

She was grateful to reach town where she could set aside her troubling thoughts. Making her simple purchases, she gathered up the mail, which consisted solely of a farm paper, and stepped back into the sunshine.

"Hi." It was Joe, leaning casually against the hitching rail, his horse snorting in his ear.

"This is a surprise." Her words were soft.

Joe tipped his head toward the blacksmith shop. "I was at the smithy when I saw you go in the store. Thought I'd wait and see if you'd like company on the walk home."

He had the disconcerting habit of turning up when she least expected him. The unexpectedness of this latest appearance drove from her mind her plan to visit Margaret, as well as every other intelligent thought, leaving her staring blank-minded and open-mouthed at him.

"What about your horse?" It was the only thing she could think of.

His eyes twinkling, he replied, "He won't mind walking with us," and turning toward the horse addressed him, "Will you, old boy?"

The horse shook his head and whinnied.

Joe had turned back to watch Bessie, his dark-eyed humor unsettling.

"See?" he said, and reached out for her basket.

She didn't remember agreeing to accompanying him yet they were walking side by side down the road toward home, the horse following in their trail. The horse nudged Joe in the shoulder and snorted. Laughing, Joe turned to face him. "Hey, cut it out," he protested. "I'm not in any hurry."

He looked down at Bessie. She swallowed and turned away from his velvet eyes.

They talked of things inconsequential, yet somehow important in that each detail revealed more of the one to the other. As they passed the groove where she had felt the urge to join the trees in worshipping God, she paused, and staring at the graceful boughs, asked, "Have you ever noticed how nature worships God?"

"Can't say as I have." Joe's voice was quiet, as if he understood she wasn't making an idle observation. As if he knew she was—without self-consciousness—about to share something special. "What do you mean?"

She was only distantly aware of his quiet consideration. Her thoughts were drawn inexplicably to the scene so rich with memories. "Look at the trees. Don't they seem to be bowing?"

Joe looked toward where she pointed. "Why, yes. Yes, they do." His voice was full of surprise.

She continued. "Watch the tips of the branches. See how they clap?" She rushed on, "And the flowers and the grass." She waved her arms. "I feel like everything is rejoicing before God."

Joe no longer looked at the trees; his eyes were fixed on her face. She laughed nervously, avoiding his gaze.

"I'm rattling on like an idiot, aren't I?" She stared at the trees, feeling his eyes still on her.

He shifted his stance. "No. Not at all." Sighing, he said, "I'm sorry if I seemed stunned, but I have never thought of nature worshipping. Now I see it everywhere. It's awesome to be surrounded by such a thing."

Turning, they resumed their homeward journey, Bessie still feeling a little shy because of her emotional explanation.

Joe broke the silence. "Bessie, thank you for telling me what you saw. I just can't get over it."

"I'm glad you appreciated it. Perhaps I've repaid in some small way your part in helping me discover God's love."

"I should say you have."

At the yard, Joe tied his horse to the corral fence, and then beamed down on her. "Let's go up the hill." He nodded in the direction of the trail.

Bessie opened her mouth to agree then hesitated. Why was she so eager? *No reason,* she decided and nodded.

In a few minutes, they stood on the crest of the hill looking down on the rolling valley, commenting on how the colors faded in layers until they disappeared into the horizon. At their feet, the ground was bright with patches of lemon yellow buffalo beans, masses of scarlet mallow the color of ripe tomatoes, and the occasional shy bluebell half hidden in the grass.

"You can see my place from here." Joe pointed past her, his arm brushing her shoulder as he pointed. She was sharply aware of the faint scent of Lifebuoy soap that seemed to be his trademark, and remembered how the smell clung to his Bible when he first gave it to her. The world was suddenly alive with sound—the high-pitched drone of unseen insects, the rustle of grass along the descent of the hill, the rattle of leaves in the nearby patch of buckbrush, the caw-caw-caw of the bold black crow as he watched them from the nearby trees. Further away, a meadowlark called in loud, clear tones, a blackbird whistled cheerfully, while high overhead, a hawk screamed. It was the music of the prairie in a lively orchestra.

"Over there." Joe's voice broke into her trance, urging her to follow the direction of his finger, and she turned her head. "A little more to the right."

There was a patch of roof through a break in the tress. "I see it."

Joe rolled back on his heels. "It's not much yet, but it has lots of potential."

As if by common consent, they sat on the grass and Joe continued telling her about his farm. Bessie could hear the pride in his voice and listened intently, eager to hear his plans and dreams.

He leaned back, turning to watch her. "Would you like to see my place someday?"

Looking across the valley to where his place lay, Bessie warned herself there wasn't any point in seeing it or in being drawn in to his dreams. She would soon be gone, and Joe would be left behind as part of her memories, even as Robert would be.

In her mind she was transported back to the day Robert had brought her to this hill to point out the beauty of the scene and extol on the wonders of the prairie. She had ignored his pleasure and refused to share his dreams, and now it was too late. She had vowed to learn a lesson from her mistake.

Turning to meet Joe's eyes, she smiled gently. "I'd like that."

"Great!" He grinned.

His whole face smiles, she thought. *Not just his mouth or even his eyes. It's his whole face.* She couldn't turn away.

Restless now, he jumped to his feet. "We'll have to make plans. Maybe Saturday. How about a picnic?"

Enthusiastic, he reached down and pulled her to her feet, almost lifting her from the ground, and sending her stumbling into his arms. He caught her shoulders and steadied her, his hands warm and gentle. She stared at him, unblinking.

He didn't release her. Instead, he let his hands slide down to the top of her arms. Eyes as dark as a moonless night, he held her gaze. A strand of hair swept across her face and, lifting his hand, he brushed it aside.

"Bessie." His voice freed her, and with a shaky laugh she stepped back.

"I must get back," she said, keeping her head turned away.

Slapping his thigh, Joe turned and looked over the scene before them. "Just one more look. I could never get too much of this view."

With those words, equilibrium was restored.

❧

He had promised to call again, but she told herself not to count on it. When he rode into the yard early the next afternoon, she stared at him in surprise. Her surprise grew as she saw that he led a second horse. Waving, he stopped at the corrals and opened the gate, taking both horses through.

Curiosity drew her to the fence to watch. Joe greeted her as he opened the gate, inviting her to step inside the corral. "Come and meet Molly," he said.

"Who's Molly?"

Catching up the reins of the smaller horse, he pulled her forward. "This is Molly, the kindest, gentlest little mare I ever met. Say hello to Molly."

Bessie looked at him warily and decided he was serious. "Hello, Molly. Nice to met you," she said to the mare.

Molly nodded her head gently.

"I hope you like her," Joe said. "You and Molly will be seeing a lot of each other."

"We will?"

"Yup. Molly is yours."

"Mine?" Couldn't she find anything more intelligent than that to say? "Why is she mine?"

"Because I give her to you."

Shaking her head, she stared up at him, the bright sky almost blinding her so that she couldn't read the expression in his eyes. Was he playing some sort of a joke?

"Yup. It's about time you learned to ride."

"It is?" She hadn't felt the need and was about to tell him so when she noticed the pleased look on his face and hesitated.

He continued, "The way it is now, you can't go anyplace you can't walk unless someone takes you in a wagon or buggy. Now if you learn to ride, you can go anywhere."

It did sound appealing.

"Molly here will be easy to ride."

What was she thinking? Mother would totally disapprove. Bessie could just picture her pursed lips and raised eyebrows. "Ladies do not ride!" Mother had never lived on the prairie. Feeling a bit defiant, Bessie made up her mind. She would learn to ride. She took a step toward Molly and hesitantly raised her hand to pat the horse's nose. Molly nodded, and Bessie was struck by the long fringe of eyelashes. She'd never thought of a horse being pretty before, but Molly was.

"Are you ready for your first lesson?"

"You mean now?"

He nodded.

Looking down at her clothes, she shook her head. "I can't ride in this."

He tipped his head as he answered. "Mrs. Kuyper does. She tucks the skirt up somehow."

Looking at him askance, she knew her mother would die of shock if she knew Bessie was having this conversation or even considering riding astride a horse. Straightening, she tucked her chin in and announced, "If Mrs. Kuyper can do it, so can I!"

"Good. Then come around to this side."

He spent the next few minutes showing her how to mount and dismount. She had watched William, Joe and others do it a hundred times and they were so graceful, while she struggled to get her leg to the other side without falling on her head, and once over, it took all her concentration to stay on top.

Finally, she managed to fling herself awkwardly into the saddle without him catching her, and he declared she was ready to ride. With visions of herself racing freely across the prairie, she clung to the saddle horn, fear and excitement making her eyes feel round as pies.

Instead, Joe picked up the reins and led her sedately around the corral. "It's important you get the feel of the horse," he said, giving her further instructions as they circled the enclosure. After a few minutes, he stopped horse and handed up the reins. "You're on your own," he announced but, his quiet voice lending her confidence, he continued to give her instructions. It was hard work and demanded total concentration.

"I think that's enough for today," announced Joe.

Licking her lips, Bessie tasted salt and realized how much effort learning to ride was going to require, yet she looked longingly across the prairie. "I thought this was going to give me some freedom," she moaned.

Joe chuckled. "In time. In time. But you'll soon find out your muscles can only take so much."

twelve

Joe had been right about the sore muscles, Bessie thought, remembering how her hips and thighs protested and her legs quivered as they practiced day after day. He had finally decided she was ready to venture further than the yard. Today was their first real ride. Due to the heat of the summer, he had suggested they wait until evening.

Bessie threw back her head and let the breeze trail across her skin cooling it from the heat of the sun's rays—still hot, though the shadows were beginning to lengthen across the prairie. For awhile, they rode side by side, without goal, then Joe suggested she let the horse out for a run. She leaned forward in the saddle, feeling the ground slip by as they covered the distance, Joe slightly ahead, but close by. It was a moment of sheer freedom for Bessie. As they reined in, she turned to Joe, laughing. "That was fun. No wonder you like to ride."

"Sure beats walking for getting a man somewhere." He drawled laconically, his face wreathed in a wide smile. "I was sure you'd enjoy it."

"I had no idea how much I would." She grinned up at him. "Thanks for teaching me. I know it took a lot of patience."

He wiggled his eyebrows. "It was my pleasure."

Glancing around her, she saw that the hill at the end of William's property was over to their right, and she reined Molly around. "Race you to the top of the hill," she called, kicking Molly in the ribs.

"Wait."

She glanced over her shoulder to see Joe pulling his horse around, then turned her attention to covering the distance. She knew she hadn't a chance to beat him, but she meant to give him a run for his money.

"You be careful." His words rumbled across the land but

133

she barely heard them over the sound of creaking leather, the thud of Molly's hooves and the wind in her hair.

Slowing as she came to the rise, Joe easily caught her, reining in as he drew even. "You could kill yourself, you know," he shouted, reaching for Molly's head, but when Bessie understood his intention, she veered aside and again kicked Molly into flight.

She arrived at the crest seconds before he did and turned to watch him race toward her. He jumped from the saddle and strode over to her, his eyes flashing. Breathing hard, he reached up, and lifted her from the saddle with ease, his big hands encircling her waist. A thrill raced upward, making her feel light-headed, and she giggled—a little gurgle of pleasure.

Dropping his hands, he glared at her, his expression fierce, but she couldn't stop grinning. Finally, he shook his head and reluctantly smiled. "I may regret having taught you how to sit a horse."

"Never!" she teased. "It will long be remembered as one of your greatest accomplishments. Why people will stare and shake their heads with wonder and whisper, 'Did you know that Joe Robertson taught her to ride?'"

He groaned. "No doubt they'll mutter a few things under their breath too."

She laughed. "You could be right."

"You scared me half to death," he grumbled. "I had visions of you falling off and killing yourself."

"It was you who taught me everything I know. Remember?" Seeing the anxiety in his eyes, she sobered, and her voice softened. "You're a good teacher."

He threw up his hands, palms outward. "I give up." He grabbed her hand and pulled her to the edge. "Besides, it's a shame to spoil such a nice evening arguing."

Keeping her hand in his, he gazed as the lowering sun painted the sky in magentas, oranges and purples of such deep hue that they could have come straight from a dye pot.

"This looks like a good place to sit." He moved to his right and smoothed the grass, throwing aside a small rock before he lowered himself to the ground. Patting the spot next to him, he invited her to join him.

Nodding silent agreement, she slipped down on the ground beside him, her emotions a tangled confusion of. . .of what? Hope, thin and uncertain, trickled through her being. She could not identify its source, and doubting its validity, quenched it to examine her other feelings. As always regret—so much regret—and guilt that refused to let her go. Her emotions were all so grey-shaded and overlapping she couldn't sort them out. All that seemed certain was the impending trip back to Toronto. Deep melancholy stole away the enjoyment of a few minutes ago.

"Isn't this one of the nicest views you've ever seen?" Joe's voice broke into her thoughts.

Without thinking, she answered, "Robert thought so." Loneliness, guilt, regret—so many things—swelled over her in consuming waves, and she sobbed.

Joe touched her hand gently then grasped it. "Ah, Bessie." It was all he said, but his voice, so full of compassion, broke a barrier in her heart and she began, brokenly, to tell him about Robert. "He came here often." Her voice cracked. "He brought me here too, wanting me to enjoy this land and see its beauty as he did." Her words fell to a whisper. " I wouldn't even look. I was too stubborn, too selfish."

She swallowed hard and Joe squeezed her hand, waiting without speaking for her to continue. "I wish. . .I wish I could go back and undo so many things." Sobs choked her and she couldn't go on.

With a muffled groan, he pulled her to his side, holding her snugly in the hollow of his shoulder. She buried her head against his chest and let the sobs wrack her body.

Finally, spent and empty, she was quiet in his embrace, feeling nothing but the beat of his heart beneath her cheek and the gentle rise and fall of his chest.

"Bessie?"

"Umm." There was no energy to move or speak.

"If we want to move forward, we must look in that direction, not backward." He paused, and still feeling numb, she let the words sink in, their meaning not touching her.

"Wouldn't Robert want you to be happy?" He spoke the words quietly, cautiously, but their affect on her was sudden and decisive. She jerked to a sitting position and turned to face him, urgency replacing every other feeling. He had reminded her of something vitally important. Something she had forgotten but that she needed to understand immediately.

"One of the last things Robert said before he—before he—one of the last things he did was make me promise to be happy. Even without him." She stared at him as if his eyes held the knowledge she needed in order to make sense of her accusing emotions.

Joe wiped the tears from her cheeks and nodded encouragingly.

She continued. "I promised him I would, but it's not that easy." Her words were firm, and she leaned toward him in her urgency. "Oh, a part of me is happy. I've accepted God's forgiveness and His peace so that part of me is able to go forward, but there's another part of me that seems frozen. Or dead. I don't know who I am or where I'm going or where I belong." She stared into Joe's dark eyes. "Who am I Joe?" Her hard words demanded an answer.

Again he wiped a tear from her cheek, his eyes so intense she found herself sinking into his soul, drawn to him in a way that made her feel as if their hearts and minds functioned as one.

"You are Bessie Macleod." His voice rang with conviction. "You are you no matter what happens in your life, or where you live. It's what's inside that counts. Nothing else."

His dark earnest eyes drew her. She drank in their intensity, wanting to believe, wanting to know who she was, wanting to believe she was somebody. Not just Robert's widow, William's sister, or the Wilson girl. Somebody in her own right.

"Bessie?" She heard the note of anxiety and tried to answer, but her thoughts were too consuming.

He dried the remains of her tears with his fingertips. Her head began to swim, and she jumped to her feet in panic, stepping away to give herself space.

"Bessie?"

"I'm fine." She nodded, keeping her face turned toward the fading sunset until she felt more calm.

The ride home was quiet; their good-byes stilted. Bessie wouldn't have been surprised if Joe didn't come again, but he called often. They frequently rode together, other times they sat and quietly visited over a cup of tea, or if the weather was hot, a glass of lemonade. Sometimes they took leisurely walks across the prairie. They did not again return to the hillside.

Today—a cloudy Saturday afternoon—Joe had arrived looking unusually nervous.

"Remember when I invited you to visit my place?" He twisted his hat in his hands.

"Of course." She had thought he'd forgotten.

"How about today?" He seemed to hold his breath.

"Today is fine."

They rode over, both admitting it was their favorite form of transportation, and the ride had been pleasantly uneventful. Joe told her more of the Kuyper family where he seemed to spend a great deal of his time. "They came from Germany with nothing but what they carried and five children. They've had another baby since they came, and now the Missus is going to have another. Fred has no experience farming and they seem to have a continual run of bad luck, though I expect some of it is of their own making. Things are tough for them."

Bessie had been about to say how good it was of Joe to help them as much as he did when Joe reined in and pointed to a slight swell in the land. "There's the house."

She gasped in pleasure, surprised at the contrast from the soddie and even William's new house. It was a small house, but nestled in amongst aspen poplar, its windows winking in the sun, it seemed sheltered and safe.

Joe was urging her forward. He helped her dismount, his hands warm about her waist, then turned to tie the horses.

They climbed a neatly graveled path to the doorway, where Joe paused and took a deep breath, then flung open the door. "Welcome to my humble abode."

Stepping over the sill, the first thing she noticed was the smell. Disinfectant permeated the place and she hid a smile. He must have given the place a thorough scrubbing in anticipation of her visit, and in fact the rooms were spotless. There were two rooms, the far one with the door ajar, revealed a wide bed covered with a colorful quilt. The room in which they stood was simple, but pleasant, with a good-sized cook stove that she envied. Four chairs huddled around a small wooden table on which was a bouquet of white daisies, brown-eyed susans, and a spray of palest blue-bells bursting out of a battered blue enamel coffee pot that had seen better days. Across the room, an oversized bent willow chair was filled with plump cushions.

"It isn't much yet," he hurriedly explained. "I designed the house so I could expand it. Someday. . ."

Why did his voice sound so urgent? He rushed on with an eagerness that made her stare at him. His eyes glowed as he pointed out where various improvements were to go.

"I'll build a kitchen with a row of windows so no matter what the season, we can look out and enjoy the scene."

Had it been a slip of the tongue that he said, "we"? Or was he referring to himself and a yet nameless bride?

He turned to face her, his eyes boring into hers. "What do you think of it?"

"It's nice." Her attention was only partially on his house. She was riveted by something seething beneath his surface that she was unable to identify. Finally she put it down to enthusiasm for his house and farm. She'd seen men besotted by land before, yet Joe's reaction seemed different. It plagued her that she couldn't quite put her finger on it.

"Are you just saying that to be polite?"

He had interpreted her distraction as disinterest in the house.

"No, of course not." She focused her attention on the room, straining to recall what he had said. "Windows looking out over the view will be nice." She rushed to the small existing window. "I can just imagine being able to watch the budding trees every spring." She noticed how Joe had planned his building to take advantage of the stand of trees. They seemed to hang over the house in a gentle embrace. She could even hear the brush of their branches against the wall. It would be a pleasant sound to wake up to. She hurried across the room to where he had indicated he would add a room for a parlor. Not a fancy one, he said, one for the family to use. "I can imagine a lovely wine-colored couch here." She pointed then turned slowly, "And over here, a big arm chair for you. Right across would be a smaller chair." She turned and saw it clearly in her mind. "A rocker for. . ." She stopped and clamped her mouth tightly closed, appalled at what she'd been about to say. "A rocker for me."

It had been so automatic, so natural, that she was forced to admit she'd been dreaming of being a part of Joe's life for some time—though when exactly it had started, she couldn't say. Why, right from the beginning, she'd felt something special. But that was impossible, she argued. Back then, she'd been a grieving widow barely able to function. *And knowing Joe was there helped me face the day,* a little voice reminded her. She loved him!

The knowledge filled her with joy, and she crossed her arms across her chest to contain it. She walked across the room and stared out the window as if appreciating the view, afraid he would read her expression.

Another thought entered her joy and splintered it.

He'd said nothing about his feelings. All the time they had spent together he'd been thoughtful and kind though their discussions had never again reached the emotional level of that evening on the hill. It seemed he cared about her feelings and tried to help her deal with her confusing emotions about Robert, and her guilt. Always he offered hope and urged her to read the Bible, but, though he was gentle and considerate and often touched her shoulder or hand, there had been nothing to indicate anything but friendship.

At one time, she'd thought that was all she wanted, but

now she knew it wouldn't be enough. It would be, at best, a meager compromise.

He crossed to the door and pulled it open, jerking her back to reality.

"Come on. I'll show you around outside." His voice seemed strange and she glanced at him. His face was sober and he kept his eyes averted. Had he guessed her thoughts?

There was no way she could tell, so she followed him outside without a word.

He showed her the barn, explaining it was temporary until he could erect a proper structure—like the ones he'd seen down east. A garden spot was worked but unplanted. "Preparing it for next year." he said. They looked at his crop, pausing at the edge of the field as he pointed out where the Kuypers lived. She could see their squat buildings about a quarter of a mile off and thought she heard the wail of a child.

All the time she followed him around, listening to his explanations, she felt she was two people. One laughing and smiling and responding to Joe's words. The other watching, observing, holding her breath, hoping for a sign from him.

It wasn't until she returned home that she began to feel like one person again. She spent much time that evening and the next morning searching the Bible, seeking God's peace and direction.

Joe had promised to call again and she'd always before anticipated his visits. Now she knew she had to settle her own feelings about him before she could comfortably face him again. She had to be content with his offer of friendship, understanding that she could enjoy it for a few weeks and then she must tuck it away in her store of memories and regrets.

Having thoroughly discussed this matter with herself and having decided on the best course of action, Bessie was annoyed that several times a day she would find herself staring into space, having completely forgotten what it was she was supposed to be doing, her mind remembering walks along the hillside, the view from Joe's house, the way his eyes darkened and flashed with his emotions, the way he moved across the corrals, the way. . .How could her mind be such a traitor?

She had to accept things the way they were. She had to get her thoughts under control before he called again, otherwise, she would embarrass the both of them.

Convinced she could do so, she was nevertheless unprepared when Joe rode into the yard, and she couldn't answer when he called out a greeting. It was as if he had suddenly materialized from her dreams, and she struggled to regain her sense of balance.

"Are you ready for the picnic?" he asked as he approached the soddie.

Picnic! That's what William had said as he drove the wagon out of the yard. She hadn't listened to his parting words and assumed he was going to visit Cecelia again. She'd plumb forgotten the plans made a couple of weeks ago for the four of them to spend the day at Salt Lake picking berries. She was to have brought cake and. . .

"Just about ready," she answered Joe, "Come in and wait while I pack it up." Thank goodness she had just finished icing a cake and there was plenty of bread for sandwiches.

The sense of being caught unprepared clung to her long after William and Cecelia returned with the wagon and they began the journey.

William pulled the wagon into the shade of the trees surrounding the small alkali lake and looked around. "What's first?"

"Let's pick berries before the sun gets any hotter," Cecelia suggested in her clear voice. Her slight accent made the syllables rise and fall in a hypnotic beat that Bessie found pleasant.

The rest agreed and headed for the thick bushes.

Bessie veered to the right, longing for some solitude to gather up the loose ends of her mind. There was a variety of berries—saskatoons, choke cherries, gooseberries, and raspberries—enough to keep them busy for several hours. Cecelia hoped to preserve some for herself and William, as well as take some to her mother.

Bessie wouldn't need any for her own use, but she didn't

mind helping Cecelia fill her needs.

Strange how things work out, she thought, remembering how she had put up preserves for William last summer, believing she would never use them herself. Yet she was still here. *Not for long, she reminded herself,* feeling as if someone had stabbed her.

If only she had more time, perhaps Joe would grow to love her as a woman. But time was running out, and she was powerless to stop its fleeting minutes.

She concentrated on the plunka, plunka of the berries dropping into her pail, and then the sound changed to a juicy plop and failed to hold her attention. She focused on the nutty blueberry taste of the small berries, and the heady smell of wild roses. Every smell, every taste, every sound was a dagger, reminding her of what she must leave behind.

Parting a bush to seek another branch laden with fruit, she saw Joe framed against the trees, his profile to her. He was absorbed in stripping berries from the branches, caring little about the amount of leaves and twigs he took with him. Bessie smiled. It would be a difficult task to sort the berries.

He dropped a handful in the bucket then picked another handful to pop in his mouth. A purple trail trickled down his fingers to his wrist and his lips were stained deep blue. As he munched the berries, he sighed aloud.

He looked like a great big boy, thoroughly lost in the pleasure of food and she stifled a giggle.

His eyes flew open and he looked about quickly until he spotted her half hidden in the leaves. For a heartbeat, he looked abashed and then he grinned and winked at her. "Don't you laugh at me," he scolded. "You wear the evidence as much as I do."

Glancing at her fingers, she discovered they were indeed bright with juice, and she wiped at her mouth, wondering if it was as stained as his.

"It's no use," he laughed. "You can't get rid of it." Then seeing her alarm, added, "It will wash off."

He let go of the branch he held and it sprang skyward as he

took a step toward her.

She studied his features, knowing she would have to fill her memories to last the rest of her life. Loneliness washed through the hollow of her heart, leaving a yearning emptiness.

He parted the bushes separating them so she could step into the tiny clearing, but she could not move. She held the sight of him in her mind wanting this moment to last a lifetime.

Then she stiffened her resolve, smiled and entered the clearing.

"You are some sight," he said, laughing, and she knew he was referring to her purple lips.

"So are you," she replied, meaning the way his smile filled every feature of his face, the dark depths of his eyes, the way he moved, the touch of his fingers.

"I can't say as it's unattractive. In fact, it looks downright appealing." He reached toward her.

"Joe," she whispered

"Joe. Bessie." Cecelia's clear voice carried through the trees. "Come join us for lunch."

Bessie jerked back a step and looked at the trampled grass at her feet and, even as she tried to ignore her own embarrassment, noticed Joe's deep sigh. Glancing up, she saw him tip his head skyward, a look of frustration marring his features, and let herself hope he was as disappointed as she to have been interrupted at that moment.

Talk at the picnic meal was mostly about the upcoming wedding.

"I'm looking forward to meeting your mother and father," she said, nodding as she spoke and glancing at Bessie before she turned her attention back to William. "They will be here soon now."

William nodded. "In two weeks."

Cecelia faced Bessie. "What are they like? William will say little, telling me I'll have to see for myself, but I would like to be more ready when they come. You tell me," she gently pleaded.

Bessie looked helplessly at William, silently begging him

to help her, but he offered no assistance. How to explain her parents to someone else? Strong, determined, upright, stiff. It sounded frightening and she had no wish to frighten Cecelia. "They are very proper," she said cautiously.

"Proper? What does that mean?" Cecelia was genuinely puzzled.

"Well, you know. They think there is a right way of doing things and everyone should understand that."

Cecelia looked alarmed.

Bessie turned on her brother. "William, how would you describe them?" *This is your responsibility,* she signaled him with her eyes.

He laughed and replied, "I couldn't begin to, which is why I have said right from the beginning she would have to wait and find out for herself."

"Now I am afraid," Cecelia moaned.

"They will love you, just as I do," William assured her and she buried her face against his shoulder.

Bessie turned away, a pang of loneliness triggered by the sight of the two of them together.

"Are you looking forward to their visit?" Joe asked her.

"Joe, I'm to return to Toronto with them. They've made arrangements." She tried to keep her voice flat, but heard the note of despair she couldn't suppress. Unable to hide her feelings, she kept her face turned away, looking out toward the white-rimmed water.

thirteen

Stunned silence greeted her words, then Joe leapt to his feet to stand looking down at Bessie.

"Bessie, I need to talk to you." His words were low and tight and Bessie wondered why she had the feeling he was struggling to control himself. He reached out and pulled her to her feet and drew her after him at a frenzied pace until they reached the same hollow in the trees they had shared before Cecelia called them.

Once there, he dropped her hand and stepped away before he turned to face her. "What did you say about going back to Toronto?" His jaw corded as he spoke through clenched teeth.

Alarmed at his fierceness, and confused by this sudden change in the man she thought she knew, Bessie answered quietly. "I'm to accompany my parents when they return." There was no point in telling him about the letters of protest she had written. They were adamant that it was inappropriate for her to stay alone in the soddie as she had suggested, and she didn't feel right about moving in with William and Cecelia. The new house was big compared to the soddie, yet in reality, still quite small. It wouldn't be fair to the newlyweds, so her parent's warnings about considering that alternative were unnecessary.

At her words, Joe whirled away and in one stride reached the edge of the clearing. Crossing his hands over his chest, he stared out through the trees. Bessie watched him silently as the frenzied hum of insects filled the air. The occasional shriek of a shore bird carried to her on the salt-laden breeze, joining with the scent of decaying fruit at her feet. Her senses were alert, warning her. . .and she tensed. But she did not know what the warning was meant for.

Joe spun on his heel and faced her. "You never told me!"

She stared at him, taken back by his accusation. "I—I—" she

faltered, and she shrugged. "I suppose I thought you knew."

With two determined strides, he closed the distance between them. "Don't you see? This changes everything. I thought I had all the time in the world and now I discover my time has almost run out." He spoke with quiet determination.

Bessie shook her head. "I don't understand."

"Bessie." Their eyes locked—she seeking to understand the way his eyes bored into hers, dark with some emotion. The dark, fluttering leaves stirred her sense of urgency. A cluster of them brushed against her arm.

"Bessie," he continued, his voice thick with emotion. "I wanted to give you more time to deal with your feelings, but I can't. Forgive me for rushing you." Reaching out, he took both her hands in his and pressed them together, wrapping his fingers around them. "Bessie, I love you."

She gasped, amazement and joy racing through her veins.

Mistaking her gasp for protest, he rushed ahead. "I know it's too soon." His voice died away.

Bessie interrupted him. "Joe, it's not too soon. I love you too."

Pulling her toward him until they were almost touching, he tipped her chin back with a curled finger. "Are you sure?" he demanded.

"I am sure."

Awe and wonder filled his expression. Gently, he cradled her face in his hands and lowered his lips to hers.

His lips were warm and gentle, and she was overwhelmed by love for this big, soft-hearted man. She put her arms around him, rejoicing in his tenderness and love for her. It was almost more than she could fathom, and joy bloomed deep in her heart, expanding, growing until it burst forth in a laugh of pure delight. Leaning back to gaze at him with a heart full of happiness, she drank in the answering pleasure in his expression.

For a slice of eternity, they looked into each others eyes, Bessie seeing mirrored in his the same wonder she felt. She noticed his eyes as never before. She could not remember seeing them so black and compelling. She watched his smile deepen, creasing his face in the way she had grown to enjoy.

Suddenly, overcome with embarrassment, she dropped her hands, but Joe caught them and pressed them to his lips.

"Ah, Bessie," he murmured. "I think I have been waiting all my life for you."

Tears wet her eyes, blurring his face, and she swallowed hard.

He ran his hand over her hair then wrapped his arms around her, crushing her to his chest where she lay content, feeling the beat of his heart matching her own, letting the rise and fall of his chest carry her on a tide of dreams.

"Bessie." his voice rumbled beneath her ear. "We need to make plans."

Tilting her head back to study him, she wondered what could possibly be important enough to break from this pleasant inertia.

Smiling, he pressed her head back to his shoulder. "I can't think when you look at me all soft-eyed like that. Bessie," he continued, "Your parents wouldn't object to you staying if you were a married woman, would they?"

"Un, unh," she murmured.

"Then let's get married."

"Umm hum." Then as she realized what he had said, she jerked back to stare at him. "Married?"

"That's what I said." He smiled at her confusion.

"You mean right now?"

He glanced around the bushes and quirked his eyebrows. "Well, probably not right now. I had in mind. . ." He brushed a hand across his cheek. "I guess I don't know what I had in mind." His eyes narrowed. "How about when your parents are here? They can see you wed and then go home knowing you'll be in good hands. Safe and sound."

"You mean right after William and Cecelia's wedding?"

"How about the next day?"

Safe and sound. That had a good ring to it. The rest of her life with Joe. Excitement mounted until she thought she would burst.

"Yes. Yes. Yes," she fairly shouted.

"My own, dear, sweet Bessie," he murmured as gently, almost reverently, he kissed her again.

They couldn't wait to tell William and Cecelia, crashing through the bushes laughing joyously as they raced toward the spot where they had left them.

"We're going to get married," they announced, grinning at each other as they said it, and proudly told their plans.

"I am so glad." Cecelia grabbed Bessie's hand. "Now you can be as happy as William and I."

Bessie sobered and met her brothers eyes, seeing his serious expression and knowing what he was thinking. What would their parents say? They had never liked surprises, but it was too late to get word to them. They would have left by the time a letter arrived, and it was a hard day's ride to the closest telegraph line.

Then William shrugged as if to say, "What can they do but accept it?" and he shook Joe's hand, congratulating him, before he gave Bessie a rare hug. Any doubts she had concerning her parents' reaction fled and she relaxed. Everything would work out.

❧

During the long hazy days that followed, they couldn't seem to see enough of each other. Joe came over as often as he could, and the times he was otherwise occupied Bessie found herself restlessly waiting for him.

Despite the heat of summer days, they often rode the long way around to the top of the hill that held so many memories for Bessie. Today they had returned to their favorite spot. Bessie sat hunched over her knees, staring out at the distance. Under the heat, the grass had dried to a parched brass color. The small patches of crop she picked out here and there across the valley wore a yellow frosting signaling the approach of harvest.

The lifeless landscape and the dry rustle of the grass filled her with uneasiness. The scream of the hawk high overhead in the brittle bright sky did nothing to ease her gnawing worry.

The wind—hot and unrelenting—caught a strand of hair and blew it across her face and fanned the beads of moisture on her upper lip.

Joe, lounging beside her, caught the errant lock of hair and tucked it behind her ear. "Bessie, my sweet, what's troubling you?"

She turned to study him. She should have know he would notice her melancholy. Since his admission of love, she had discovered a deeply affcctionate, gently sensitive man. Now he was looking at her, his eyes bright with concern, and she turned her mind to answering his question.

"I'm just being silly," she admitted. "But I'm dreading facing my parents."

Smiling, he tweaked her nose. "That's a relief. I thought you were having second thoughts about marrying me."

She grasped her hand to her lips, fervently kissing his palm. "Never."

At that, she half expected him to hug her and kiss her, but he remained motionless beside her, still studying her expression. She watched the emotions play on his face and knew he was seeing more than she was confessing. She tipped her chin toward him, as he asked, "Is there something you haven't told me?"

With a deep sigh, she turned to look across the valley, seeing not the patches of yellowed grass and darker crop. Instead, she was seeing herself as a girl growing up, always feeling she couldn't do anything right. Never quite living up to her parents' expectations. She struggled to find the words to tell Joe what she was feeling. "It's that I've always felt so incompetent around them, as if everything I do is inappropriate, or foolish. When I think about them coming, I begin to feel like a little girl again, always trying, never succeeding. I don't want to feel this way, but I do. It makes me angry."

There she had finally admitted it, not only to Joe, but to herself. Her parents made her feel young and foolish, and she didn't like it. But what could she do? They would be here in two days time. There was no escaping it. She wanted to scream and cry. Jumping to her feet, she paced across the grass.

Joe rose more slowly and watched her, his eyes dark with concern.

"Bessie, come here." He held out his arms.

Turning, she hesitated but a moment before she fled to the safety of his embrace.

He held her, not speaking, not demanding anything, until she began to relax.

"Bessie, my sweet Bessie. You have nothing to fear. You are one of the bravest, strongest women I have ever met. You've faced things lots of people never have, and you've grown better for it."

She raised her face to study him, drinking in the love written in his eyes. "What things do you mean?"

"You came west with a sick husband and nursed him faithfully, ignoring your own fears of the dark soddie."

When she stiffened in protest, he shook her gently before pulling her back into his arms. "You hate the soddie. I know you do."

She nodded against his shoulder, though in truth, she seldom thought about it any more. It was only on damp, dark days—days that shut out the sunshine and invited the spiders out—that the terrors returned.

"That's not all," he continued. "You had to deal with the death of your husband, learning to live without him in a cold, unforgiving land."

Again she wanted to protest, but she knew he was right. How did he know all these things when she had never told anyone?

"And the hardest thing of all. You had to deal with your guilt."

He was right. She had no reason to feel like a silly child before her parents. She was a mature grownup and had proved it by dealing with adversity in a positive way. He had only forgotten one thing. "I couldn't have done it without you," she whispered, looking into his dark eyes. "It was you who showed me the way. It was you who told me of God's love." Her voice broke. Tears stung the corners of her eyes. He'd brought so much into her life—heavenly love, and his own sweet love. Her heart was too full to contain it, and she choked back a sob. "Joe, I love you so much."

Tenderly, he wiped the tears from her cheeks, pressing a kiss to the dampened spots. "My sweet, sweet Bessie."

Her worries about the impending parental visit were forgotten.

For now.

જ

Joe had come over the morning after Mother and Father arrived. Together they had confessed their love.

"Mother, Father," Bessie had said. "We want to get married the day after William and Cecelia. All the arrangements have been made. We have the license and the preacher has agreed to stay the extra day."

"I promise to take good care of her," Joe added.

"This seems very sudden." Lips pursed, eyes narrowed with disapproval, Mother made her opinion clear, even without the words she uttered.

"Your mother and I need time to think about this," was all her father said and she knew she had been dismissed.

Nothing more had been said.

The next day had been busy with last minute preparations for the wedding, but now that was behind them. William and Cecelia were safely married and had ridden away to their new house.

Bessie looked around for Joe. He had hovered close to her side, never out of sight throughout the ceremony and the tea that followed, but now she couldn't find him.

Wandering past the tables as Cecelia's younger sisters cleaned up, Bessie searched the lingering groups for Joe. Being a head taller than most men, he was usually easy to spot, but still she was unable to find him.

Going further afield, she thought she caught a glimpse of his figure down by the horses and headed in that direction. It was then she saw her father and Joe facing each other. Father was in his best court room stance, a raised finger in Joe's face. Bessie could see Joe disputing something with him. Picking up her skirts, she ran toward them. What was Father saying? She had a dreadful feeling. The two men stared at each other, and even from where she was, Bessie could sense the stubborn confrontation between them. Suddenly Joe spun on his heel, and with one swift movement, was in his saddle. Jerking the reins, he spurred his horse into a run.

She was running, running, running, but the distance between them widened. "Joe," she screamed, but he didn't hear. He didn't turn. He didn't slow his pace. Her voice died to a wail and she stared after him.

What had her father said? Where was Joe going? She had missed him throughout the day for they always seemed to be separated by another person, or a table, or a chair, and she longed to be close enough to touch, but he had ridden out without even saying good-bye.

"Come along, Bessie." She hadn't seen her father approach, yet he stood at her side, urging her toward the church.

Mother joined them immediately, and Bessie wondered if she had seen the whole thing. Nor did she miss the look her parents exchanged. Again, warning signals flashed through her brain. What was going on?

"We'll be leaving right away," Father announced and she noticed the carriage he had rented, standing ready.

"I. . ." She'd been about to say she had to say good-bye to Joe, but Joe had already gone. She climbed obediently into the carriage. *Where did he go?* her brain screamed.

She could do little more than mumble vague responses to Mother and Father's comments about the wedding as they journeyed homeward.

As they turned into the yard, she sat up and stared. The wagon was drawn up before the soddie and loaded, a young man she recognized as from the livery barn in town leaned against the wheel, apparently waiting.

Before the buggy stopped rolling, she jumped to the ground, and hurried toward the wagon. "These are Robert's boxes.

Why are they in this wagon?" Circling the end gate, she saw more of Robert's possessions. Her bag! Dread settled in the pit of her stomach as she turned toward her parents.

They waited beside the buggy, their expressions hard.

"What is going on?" Bessie ground out the words as she marched toward them. "Why are my things in the wagon? Who did this?"

"Now be calm, dear," her mother implored, taking off her gloves in what seemed to Bessie to be military precision. Suddenly, she saw her Mother as she really was. Controlling, critical.

"Where's Joe? What did you do to Joe?" she demanded of her father.

Stepping forward, he drew himself up and puffed out his chest. "I explained a few facts to him, just as I am about to do to you." He would not allow her to interrupt, silencing her protests with a look. "This business between you is foolishness."

"No," she managed before he continued, not so much as blinking at her objection.

"You, my dear child, have been hoodwinked. All this talk about God and being in love. You don't know what you want. You've always been easily influenced by those stronger than you."

Watching him lean back, she knew he was about to deliver a lecture.

She was no longer a child. She was a mature woman, able to reason for herself. No one had hoodwinked her as Father said. She had thought things through carefully and she had made up her mind. She knew what she wanted.

"What on earth were you thinking?" her mother sniffed. "Imagine what people think. Why Robert hasn't been dead a year, and here you are already planning to remarry. Could you not have waited until his grave was cold before you started seeing another man?"

Bessie staggered as if she had been struck. Memories of how cold his body had felt in her arms that last night assailed her.

Then they had laid him in the cold ground. She had begged William not to do it, but he had pulled her aside and held her close. Cold. Cold. Cold. How the cold had seeped into her soul. His death had been her fault. She couldn't argue with that. Had she thought she could forget it?

"We are leaving for home right now." Her father made the announcement while her mother propelled her toward the soddie.

"We left out a travelling outfit. Hurry and change," her mother ordered, and Bessie obeyed automatically. She glanced around the soddie as she unbuttoned her dress. It seemed empty with all her things gone. When had they found time to pack everything? Prior to the wedding, while she had helped Cecelia, she answered herself.

She took her time changing, hoping that Joe would ride into the yard and make everything well again. *I killed Robert,* her brain screamed, *what right do I have to happiness?*

Her mother guided her to the wagon. Her father helped her climb up. She moved slowly, without a will of her own. As they headed down the road, she turned to look at the hill where she and Joe had spent so much time. A big man on a big horse was silhouetted motionless against the sky. Bessie almost choked on her tongue and tears blurred her vision. Across the distance she could feel him reaching for her. Blinking to clear her vision, she strained for another glimpse of him but a turn in the trail hid the hill. A silent moan wailed through her heart.

fourteen

Life became a blur of sounds and sights for Bessie. She moved woodenly, eating, retiring to her bedroom, rising, helping with the household duties only if someone suggested she should. She had lost all ability to direct her own affairs. She could not think, and would not feel.

She did not remember the train ride back to Toronto, nor returning to her childhood bedroom. She knew old friends and acquaintances called, but she could not recall what they said or why they had come, nor whether she had responded to their words.

It had been late summer when her plans and dreams had been ripped from her. It seemed cold now, and she wondered vaguely if winter had arrived, but stared out the living room window without seeing any of the details of nature. It didn't matter. Nothing mattered.

"This has gone on long enough!" Her mother's sharp voice behind her made her jump and clutch her hands to her throat. "Young lady, it is time you snapped out of this sulk and got back to normal."

"Mother, I'm trying," she protested weakly, piqued at being called sulky. Did Mother have no idea of what it felt like to have your whole life ripped from you?

Mother snorted. "Moping about the place is not trying. Now you come with me." She marched up the stairs, Bessie trailing after her. They stepped inside Bessie's bedroom, and Bessie gasped.

"What have you done?" Packing boxes lined the floor.

"I've had some of your things—yours and Robert's— moved in here so you can go through them." She stood in front of the boxes. "You need to decide how to dispose of these things." She fluttered her hand. "I'm sure you'll want to keep some of it as mementos, and that sort of thing, but I'm quite certain you can give some to Robert's mother, or perhaps donate his books to a library." Her brisk steps pausing at the doorway, she flung over her shoulder. "You should have no trouble finishing these few crates this afternoon."

Bessie stared after her, wanting to vent her rage in a loud scream. She had just been ordered to dispose of her dead husband's belongings like so much garbage. Bitterness welled up from her stomach and she choked it back. Was this not the same woman who had berated her for appearing to forget his death with unseemly haste?

She walked over to the boxes and ran her fingers along the edge of the top one. It all seemed so backward. Mother was concerned with appearances, not what was in the heart. Bessie would never forget Robert, would love him always, but she felt it was right to get on with her life. Joe understood. At least she had thought he did. Shaking her head, she clamped her mind shut against any more thought of Joe, knowing the only way to avoid the gut-wrenching pain that came with every remembrance was to studiously avoid thinking of him.

She turned her attention to the crates. The tops had been pried loose. Determined to keep her hands busy and her mind numb, she lifted the boards and began pulling out volume after volume of law books. Mother was right. She had no need of these. It was too bad she couldn't have left them with Mr. Scofield, she thought, knowing there was a shortage of books on the prairies.

Why not? she decided. Mother had said she was to decide what to do with them. She'd simply give instructions for them to be shipped to his address.

She repacked the first box and turned her attention to the next. It contained more of the same, plus bundles of letters. Quickly, she sorted them. The ones from Mrs. Macleod she would return. She had no desire to even read them, but knew Robert's mother would cherish them.

Others, and the periodicals Robert had collected, she put in a pile to be burned.

The third crate contained more miscellaneous possessions. She unwrapped Robert's shaving gear, lingering over the scent, treasuring the memories she had of him shaving in front of the small round mirror, his strokes so precise and measured. She thought of keeping the things, then decisively added them to the pile for Mrs. Macleod. Bessie had her memories. Nothing would ever take them away. Robert's mother needed the tangible evidence of her son's life.

She turned back to her unpacking. On the bottom of the crate lay the three journals Robert had used while they were in Alberta. Bessie lifted them out with both hands and sank to the floor, pressing the black volumes to her mouth. These, more than anything else, brought Robert so close she felt she could almost reach out and touch him. They had been so much a part of his every day life. Pictures of him bent over the page, laboriously trying to sketch one of the flowers or writing his voluminous notes filled her mind. How often she had silently scoffed at his meticulous habit, wondering what there was to record about the prairies. What had he found noteworthy?

Curiosity overcame her sense of reluctance, and checking the dates on the covers, she opened the first volume, skimming the pages. It was mostly lists. Lists of "Animals Seen For The First Time" with notations as to their coloring and habits, lists of "Supplies William Keeps On Hand," a detailed list of the soddie's contents and where everything was kept. She had glimpsed some of his previous journals and knew they too, were mostly lists. She continued. At first, there was nothing more than lists, but toward the end, she saw he had begun to add comments and sketches. Quickly, she picked up the second volume and saw the lists had been almost completely replaced by descriptive paragraphs.

She held the first two volumes in her hands turning from one to the other. Why this change in his style? What did it mean? To the casual observer, it would seem more usual to use the second method—descriptive paragraphs—than the lists, but she knew it wasn't usual for Robert, and had always wondered if his list-making was one way he had of assuring himself he had some control of his life when so often his poor health made him feel he had none.

She skimmed through the rest of volume two, smiling at the sketch of the soddie. He had made it appear even less appealing than it was—if that were possible.

> *I think I have grown new depths in this wide vast country.*

It was a simple enough statement, but its impact made Bessie blink. As far as she could tell, it was the first time he had revealed any feelings in his writings, and she knew that one statement explained the change in his writing habits.

Reaching the end of volume two, she scooped up the third book, anxious to learn more about Robert as revealed through his notes.

> *Bessie thinks I'm better, and indeed I appear to be. But I know I'm not. I doubt I will make it through the cold of winter. At times my lungs hurt for no apparent reason and I'm forced to admit they are simply worn out.*

She looked at the date—August tenth—and thought back to their last summer. She had been so sure he was healed and they could return to Toronto. She had dreamed of life in the city, filled with friends, babies, conveniences. It all seemed so shallow and selfish in light of Robert's knowledge about his health.

> *Mr. Scofield assures me I can face death knowing it is simply a passing from this life to the next. We must choose our destiny though, he says. He believes God offers us heaven as a gift. Mr. S. says as sinners we can't be allowed in but God has made a way*

through the cross. I think I am beginning to believe.

A tear dropped to the page and she blotted it before it could blur the writing. Robert had heard about God's love. It quelled a regret she had carried all summer. She must write Mr. Scofield and thank him.

Continuing to read, she turned page after page until she came to an entry for September twelve.

> *I sense time is growing short though why I should feel this way, I cannot say for I feel better than I ever have in my life.*

She skipped some description searching for more of Robert.

> *I am ready to meet my Maker. My only concern is for Bessie. She is young and beautiful.*

Bessie gasped. Robert had never told her that. She sobbed, pressing her knuckles to her lips, so she could continue.

> *I cannot bear to think of B. as a sorrowing widow. She is so full of life and life is meant for living and loving.*

She could not go on. Robert himself had wished for her to continue living and loving. She knew he would wish her happiness with Joe.

Where was Joe? He hadn't so much as written her one letter.

Her eyes narrowed. Father had a way with words. Somehow he'd managed to convince Joe that their love was a mistake. Or perhaps Joe had reached that conclusion on his own.

She tucked the journals away for safekeeping as fresh tears flooded her cheeks. Sinking to the edge of her bed, she quietly rocked back and forth as she sobbed. How could she bear the pain of losing Joe as well as Robert?

❧

The next day, Mother had three more crates brought in with the same instructions.

These boxes, Bessie soon discovered, contained an even wider variety of goods. It was in the second that she found Joe's Bible. She gasped. All this time, she believed it had been left behind in the soddie, and she thought she would never see it again. Tenderly, she lifted it to her lips, drowning in her memories.

Everything seemed so intertwined—the Bible, Joe's talks that had lead her to discovering God's love, and Joe himself.

Lifting her head, she gazed out the lace-covered windows, seeing nothing but the sky. She needed to sort out her tangled thoughts.

Finally, with a deephearted sigh at her foolishness, she admitted she had put God and Joe into one shell, believing their love was one and the same.

If she couldn't have Joe's love, she couldn't have God's love, or so, in her confusion, she had thought, and by her own foolishness deprived herself of the one steady source of comfort she could count on—God and his unfailing love for her.

It was as if she were back to the early days of spring, struggling to survive in a sea of sorrow.

Remember, the sun is shining even when you can't see it. Joe's words rang in her head, taking her back to that first day when he had told her about God's love. Through his help, and especially through the gift of this Bible—she clutched it to her—she had indeed discovered God's love, as well as peace and forgiveness.

She opened the pages to the Psalms, quickly finding her favorite passages, and allowed calming peace to flow through her.

The light was fading when she looked up again.

She shook her head. Why had she allowed guilt to cripple her? Yes, she knew she bore some responsibility for Robert's last illness, but she knew Robert would not have accused her.

His journals revealed that he knew his time was running out—with or without their quarrel.

More importantly, she knew God forgave her.

All that had kept her from writing Joe these past torturous weeks, begging him to explain what had happened, was her guilt, accusingly telling her she didn't deserve the love of another man.

Rising stiffly to her feet, she crossed to her writing desk and pulled out pen, ink and paper.

> *Dear Joe,*
>   *I'm not sure what Father said to you after William and Cecelia's wedding, but I want you to know how I feel.*

She lifted her pen and stared at the words. Why hadn't Joe written her himself? Could it be that he had changed his mind? She crumpled the letter and threw it in a basket.

The clock at her bedside ticked away unnoticed as she stared at the now empty writing surface. Did she want to live without Joe?

⟡

All through the following days, while the first snow fell and cold held the land in its grip, and past the events of the Christmas season, Bessie searched for the answer to that question. Only this time, she did not look into her bruised and battered heart for the solution. She looked in the Bible.

Life went on around her, and to her friends and family she appeared to be partaking of the activities—joining in family celebrations during the holidays, attending a small church close by, laughing and smiling and talking. She alone knew that she was desperate to find solace for her sad and lonely heart.

As the days lengthened and the sun grew warmer, she found a growing measure of peace. It was easier to get up each morning with a smile, and find small pleasures to delight in.

She reminded herself that she was fortunate to have enjoyed

the love of two good men, no matter how brief the time, rather than to suffer perpetual loneliness, and she thought of some of the spinster ladies she knew. The knowledge was mental right now, but she hoped someday it would also be an emotional response.

Could she live without Joe? The question continued to haunt her.

In time, perhaps she would learn to enjoy life. For now, she was content to let God's peace rule deep in her heart.

Yet the ache would not go away—every day, a dull throb at the back of her eyes, a hollowness in the pit of her stomach that would not be relieved.

Occasionally, some small memory would catch her totally unprepared—like the scent of Lifebuoy soap as she passed a stranger on the street—and she'd have to press her fingers to her lips to keep from crying out. Her heartbeats would send sharp pains into her chest as she struggled to regain control.

Each time this happened, Bessie renewed her efforts to resume a normal life. She had no choice. She had to accept that Joe's love was not to be. Otherwise she surely would have heard from him by now. A letter, a message—something.

There was nothing except a few brief words in Margaret's letters. Margaret carefully avoided mentioning the broken relationship between Joe and Bessie, but her letters often contained references to the neighbors—Joe among them.

Picking up the latest one, she read the bit about Joe.

> *Joe was away for a few days and we wondered where he had gone. It seems he helped widowed Emily Houghten move back to her parents' home. I think I told you about the accident her husband was killed in.*

She laid the letter down again. At least there would be no more restless waiting for a letter from Joe. No more wondering if he had changed his mind. It seemed he had found another widow to fill his days.

The news should have eased her mind. Instead, it felt as if someone were sucking her innards out through her toes and she was forced to grab the chair and fall into it as her knees turned to mush. For a long time, she could do nothing but concentrate on her breathing, but at last her mind cleared and she reread Margaret's letter jerking her eyes over the passage containing Joe's name.

Picking up her pen, she began a reply, dwelling on church and family activities, carefully avoiding any mention of her pain and disappointment. Only once did she hint at how much she longed to be back in Alberta when she casually asked if the crocuses were in bloom, and were they as beautiful as ever?

Glancing at the clock, she saw that it was time to leave. The ladies at the church had planned a picnic this afternoon.

"Just to celebrate spring," the unofficial leader had said and everyone agreed it was reason enough. Bessie had offered her help.

Blotting the letter, she set it aside to finish later.

The afternoon was ideal for a picnic. The ladies had filled jugs with red and yellow tulips and sprays of apple blossoms. The children revelled in the warm sunshine. One of the ladies had come up with the idea of having a "ball party," and balls of every sort had been brought. The yard was a frenzy of balls and squealing, laughing children.

Bessie brought out another pot of coffee and refilled cups as the older people sauntered by.

Suddenly, from behind, someone grabbed her shoulders and growled, "Bessie."

Joe. It was her first thought, hope overcoming reason with frightening ease, and she spun around to face the man.

"Peter!" For a moment she felt a surge of bitter disappointment then joy at seeing her favorite cousin swept over her and she flew into his arms to be swept off in a swinging embrace.

He set her down and pushed her away to look into her face

and ask, "How are you, Bess?"

"I'm fine. When did you get here? Aunt Grace thought you'd be another day or two."

Pulling her arm through his, he headed toward the laden tables. "Let's eat while we talk." As he filled his plate, he explained, "I made better time than I planned. Besides, I was more anxious to get home than I thought I would be." He continued to pile his plate until it threatened to overflow.

Laughing, she said, "I see you still have a dainty appetite."

"When did you begin to say no to sweets?" He wiggled his eyebrows, frowning mockingly at the lone cookie on her plate. She shrugged and turned away, heading toward a quiet spot in the yard.

Finding a place along the fence, they talked and laughed and caught up with what had happened to them both since Peter had left for England three years ago.

Setting aside his now-empty plate, Peter turned to study her, his expression suddenly serious. "Bess, I wish I could have been here for you. When Mother wrote me, I almost turned around and came home. I would never have gone if I'd known what was ahead for you."

She nodded, touched by his concern. "I'm fine now. Older and wiser, of course, but fine." It was her turn to study his face for signs of sorrow or despair. "How about you? You're sure about coming back?" He had gone to visit his grandparents, perhaps to stay and help them run their farm, but he wrote that he had decided the old country didn't suit him and he was returning to Canada.

He smiled. "Apart from leaving Grandma and Poppa, it wasn't a hard decision. You're really well?"

Smiling, she nodded, and he hugged her to his chest.

"You better be," he warned her teasingly.

As she pulled away, she thought she caught the scent of Lifebuoy soap and jerked toward the sidewalk. Did she catch the fleeting figure of a large man? Joe? It was a silent, despairing cry and she turned back to see Peter studying her with narrowed eyes.

"I thought I saw someone." She laughed nervously, promising herself this would be the last time—the very last time—she would let her senses bolt to attention over some imagined suggestion that Joe was close by.

❧

There was no one home when she returned and she welcomed the solitude, bringing her letter down to the front parlor to finish. She penned a sentence or two about Peter's return, but all she wanted to write was, Is Joe seeing Emily Houghten? Has he forgotten me? She knew she would never put her burning questions on paper, and she set aside the pen, unable to continue.

A yearning restlessness made it impossible to relax and she began to pace the room.

If only she'd never met Joe! Then her dreams could not have been dashed to pieces. Dealing with Robert's death had been hard, but having Joe ripped from her, knowing he was out there somewhere, perhaps with someone else to love, was pain that would not be soothed. Better to have never met him, she told herself again, feeling the pain deepen even as she repeated the words. She had become a different person when she and Joe—fell in love. The words screamed inside her head.

How could he have declared love so fervently and then forgotten so soon?

The rapping of the door knocker jerked her back to the present and she hurried to answer it, telling herself she was grateful for the interruption.

If only she could find some answers! But only Joe could supply those and she was destined to never see him again.

With those thoughts filling her mind, she pulled open the door. Giving a cry of alarm, she fell back.

"Joe!" Her voice was a tight squeak.

"Hello, Bessie."

"Joe." This time her voice more normal, and she prayed he would not hear the desperation she felt.

"I have a message for your parents. Are they in?"

"Umm, yes." She shook her head. "I mean no." It must be a

dream. But if it's a dream why is he standing there so stiff and serious? He should have been sweeping her up in his arms, kissing her and declaring he would never let her out of his sight again. Instead, he was staring at her, his dark eyes so distant she felt like they were strangers. Swallowing, she forced herself to answer calmly. "No. They aren't home. Could I take a message for them?"

He rubbed his hand across his chin. She wanted to turn around and run, but she couldn't tear her eyes away from his hand, rasping back and forth across his whiskers.

He dropped his hand and she blinked away her shattered dreams.

"William wanted them to know he and Cecelia are expecting a baby in September. Cecelia is well." He could have been a telegraph messenger, he delivered his words so flatly. He made as if to turn, and she realized he was about to leave.

Did he have nothing to say to her? Surely he hadn't come all this way simply to deliver a message that could have easily come by letter.

She couldn't let him go yet. She needed an explanation from him.

The letter to Margaret.

"Wait," she cried. "Can you come in and wait a minute? I was just finishing a letter to Margaret. Perhaps you can take it back for me." She didn't even know if he was planning to go back, but it didn't matter.

"I was just asking her if the crocuses were out. Maybe you can tell me. Are they?" She was babbling, but she couldn't stop.

He stepped into the hall and stood waiting. "They were just beginning when I left," he answered, still unsmiling.

Tears stung her eyes and she turned to the desk, pulling out a chair and blindly dropping into the seat. She couldn't let him see her cry. Staring at the envelope, she was unable to see to address it and wiped her eyes to clear her vision.

The sound of Joe clearing his throat sent a spear of alarm through her and she quickly bent to her task.

"I trust you are happy now." His voice was strangely tight.

Why should he ask about my happiness? she thought, a spurt of anger instantly drying her tears. Didn't he know how much it hurt to have him withdraw his love? Keeping her attention on the pages as she folded them and inserted them in the envelope, she answered without turning around. "I'm learning to be." Steeling herself to be strong, she turned and handed him the letter. "Thank you."

Turning the letter round and round in his big hands, he made no move to leave.

Please go, she begged silently. Quickly while I can still hold back the tears.

Instead, he cleared his throat again and raised his head to search her eyes. "I saw you at the picnic this afternoon."

A jolt raced through her. It hadn't been her imagination—but why hadn't he made his presence known?

"You were enjoying the company of a nice-looking young man. I hope you will be happy."

She couldn't wait for him to leave her alone with her grief. Yet she was torn by a desire to grab him and demand answers—answers she didn't think she could stand to hear. Her confusion made her lips stiff as she answered him. "You must mean my cousin Peter. Yes, I'm sure he'll make life a little more interesting now he's back."

A jolt raced through Joe and his eyes brightened. For a moment she wondered as to its cause, but she couldn't dwell on it for she was about to break in half and had to concentrate on keeping her emotions under control until he left.

"Please give my love to William and Cecelia. Thank you for bringing their good news." Turning, she reached for the door, anxious to hurry him away.

"Bessie."

She froze at the sound of her name on his lips. It was a sound she had longed to hear for so many months she decided she must be dreaming again.

"Bessie?" There it was again. Soft, pleading. Slowly, feeling as if it were not she, but someone she was watching from the corner, she turned.

He met and held her gaze, his eyes searching hers for what she did not know.

"Was that your cousin Peter I saw you with this afternoon?"

She nodded, unable to make her voice function.

"I saw you and thought you had found someone else."

She shook her head, her tongue still useless.

"I wanted to give you time to sort things out. You'd had so much to deal with and I knew your parents were right. It was too soon after the loss of Robert for you to know for sure how you felt."

Her voice returned with a vengeance. "You make me sound like I don't have a brain. Do you know how many things I dealt with on my own? Not just Robert's death. I lived in a dark, damp soddie that made my skin crawl, but I learned to deal with it. I learned to deal with all the hardships and inconveniences of the barren land. On my own, I examined the truths in God's word and on my own, made my choice. I examined my heart and knew it what was right for me. I've known what I wanted for a long while. I didn't need time." *I needed you.* She strangled back the words, afraid of opening up her wound to the air.

"Bessie." He shook his head. "I never meant to hurt you and I have." His jaw muscles corded. "I thought. . .and then I saw you this afternoon and. . ." He broke off, his eyes clouding.

Tears blurred her vision. "I don't need more time," she whispered.

"I've thought about you all winter, hoping you would still care. When my letters were returned unanswered. . ."

"Your letters," she gasped. "You wrote me letters?"

"Every day for six weeks. I never heard back and then finally the letters were returned unopened. I was sure you had changed your mind. . ." His voice cracked and he lifted his head, his throat working as he swallowed hard. "But I had to hear it from your lips to believe it. Then this afternoon. . ."

He couldn't continue.

She wanted to cry out at the injustice of it. All this time, she had thought how readily he forgot, and he thought she had returned his letters. It would be difficult to forgive her parents for hiding the truth from her.

"I couldn't forget you though I tried at first. Then I didn't try any more. I saw your face when I dug the barn out of the snow. I remembered every walk we took and every word we said. I remembered the way your face changed when you talked about the future. I clung to every shred of memory, hoping it would be enough." He shook his head. "It was never enough." Sighing, he pulled her closer. "Bessie. I love you. I always will."

Her chest tightened around her heart until her ribs vibrated with each heartbeat. She pressed toward him, longing to be in his arms, but he held her away.

"Tell me you still love me." He searched her eyes hungrily.

The hollowness inside her overflowed with bubbling joy. "I love you, Joe Robertson. With all my heart. Now and forever."

With a shout of joy, he crushed her in his arms. Her longings were thoroughly met.

❧

Two weeks later they were married at a simple gathering at the church she had been attending. The trip back to Alberta passed in a blur as they exalted in their love for each other and the assurance of being together for the rest of their lives.

"I had to keep busy," Joe explained as they stood before the addition to his house. Bessie knew she would have a wide pleasant view from the windows. In her mind, she had seen it many times already.

"It's beautiful," she nodded, looking around. Not only the house, but the sky, the sweeping land, everything. How could she have ever thought the prairies were vast and lonely? They were warm and welcoming today.

Laughing against her cheek, Joe swept her into his arms

and carried her across the threshold.

She knew his love had everything to do with the welcome she felt. She had come home.

A Letter To Our Readers

Dear Reader:

In order that we might better contribute to your reading enjoyment, we would appreciate your taking a few minutes to respond to the following questions. When completed, please return to the following:

Rebecca Germany, Managing Editor
Heartsong Presents
P.O. Box 719
Uhrichsville, Ohio 44683

1. Did you enjoy reading *The Sun Still Shines?*
   ❑ Very much. I would like to see more books
     by this author!
   ❑ Moderately
     I would have enjoyed it more if _____
     _____

2. Are you a member of **Heartsong Presents**? ❑Yes ❑No
   If no, where did you purchase this book? _____
   _____

3. What influenced your decision to purchase this
   book? (Check those that apply.)

   ❑ Cover   ❑ Back cover copy

   ❑ Title   ❑ Friends

   ❑ Publicity   ❑ Other_____

4. How would you rate, on a scale from 1 (poor) to 5
   (superior), the cover design? _____

_____

5. On a scale from 1 (poor) to 10 (superior), please rate the following elements.

___Heroine   ___Plot

___Hero   ___Inspirational theme

___Setting   ___Secondary characters

6. What settings would you like to see covered in **Heartsong Presents** books?_____

_____

_____

7. What are some inspirational themes you would like to see treated in future books?_____

_____

_____

8. Would you be interested in reading other **Heartsong Presents** titles?   ❑ Yes   ❑ No

9. Please check your age range:
   ❑ Under 18   ❑ 18-24   ❑ 25-34
   ❑ 35-45   ❑ 46-55   ❑ Over 55

10. How many hours per week do you read? _____

Name _____

Occupation_____

Address_____

City_____ State_____ Zip _____

101
Ways to Say
"*I Love You*"

How do you say I love you? By sending love notes via overnight delivery. . .by watching the sunrise together. . .by calling in "well" and spending the day together. . .by sharing a candlelight dinner on the beach. . .by praying for the man or woman God has chosen just for you.

When you've found *the one*, you can't do without *one hundred and one ways* to tell them exactly how you feel. Priced to be the perfect subsitute for a birthday card or love note, this book fits neatly into a regular envelope. Buy a bunch and start giving today!

Specially Priced!
Buy 10 for only $9.97!
or 5 for only $4.97!

48 pages, Paperbound, 3½" x 5½"

·········· Presents ··········

Great Inspirational Romance at a Great Price!

Heartsong Presents books are inspirational romances in contemporary and historical settings, designed to give you an enjoyable, spirit-lifting reading experience. You can choose wonderfully written titles from some of today's best authors like Peggy Darty, Sally Laity, Tracie J. Peterson, Colleen L. Reece, Lauraine Snelling, and many others.

When ordering quantities less than twelve, above titles are $2.95 each.
Not all titles may be available at time of order.

Hearts♥ng Presents
Love Stories Are Rated G!

That's for godly, gratifying, and of course, great! If you love a thrilling love story, but don't appreciate the sordidness of some popular paperback romances, **Heartsong Presents** is for you. In fact, **Heartsong Presents** is the *only inspirational romance book club*, the only one featuring love stories where Christian faith is the primary ingredient in a marriage relationship.

Sign up today to receive your first set of four, never before published Christian romances. Send no money now; you will receive a bill with the first shipment. You may cancel at any time without obligation, and if you aren't completely satisfied with any selection, you may return the books for an immediate refund!

Imagine. . .four new romances every four weeks—two historical, two contemporary—with men and women like you who long to meet the one God has chosen as the love of their lives. . .all for the low price of $9.97 postpaid.

To join, simply complete the coupon below and mail to the address provided. **Heartsong Presents** romances are rated G for another reason: They'll arrive *Godspeed!*